LABYRINTH
OF THE LOST

LABYRINTH OF THE LOST

ANDY CLARK

BLACK LIBRARY

A BLACK LIBRARY PUBLICATION

First published in Great Britain in 2016 by
Black Library
Games Workshop Ltd
Willow Road
Nottingham NG7 2WS UK

10 9 8 7 6 5 4 3 2 1

Produced by Games Workshop in Nottingham

Labyrinth of the Lost © Copyright Games Workshop Limited 2016. Labyrinth of the Lost, Warhammer Quest Silver Tower, GW, Games Workshop, Black Library, Warhammer, Warhammer Age of Sigmar, Stormcast Eternals, and all associated logos, illustrations, images, names, creatures, races, vehicles, locations, weapons, characters, and the distinctive likenesses thereof, are either ® or TM, and/or © Games Workshop Limited, variably registered around the world.
All Rights Reserved.

A CIP record for this book is available from the British Library.

ISBN 13: 978 1 78496 192 3
Product code: 60040281054

No part of this publication may be reproduced, stored in a retrieval system, or transmitted in any form or by any means, electronic, mechanical, photocopying, recording or otherwise, without the prior permission of the publishers.

This is a work of fiction. All the characters and events portrayed in this book are fictional, and any resemblance to real people or incidents is purely coincidental.

See Black Library on the internet at

blacklibrary.com

Find out more about Games Workshop
and the world of Warhammer at

games-workshop.com

Printed and bound by CPI Group (UK) Ltd, Croydon, CR0 4YY

From the maelstrom of a sundered world, the Eight Realms were born. The formless and the divine exploded into life.

Strange, new worlds appeared in the firmament, each one gilded with spirits, gods and men. Noblest of the gods was Sigmar. For years beyond reckoning he illuminated the realms, wreathed in light and majesty as he carved out his reign. His strength was the power of thunder. His wisdom was infinite. Mortal and immortal alike kneeled before his lofty throne. Great empires rose and, for a while, treachery was banished. Sigmar claimed the land and sky as his own and ruled over a glorious age of myth.

But cruelty is tenacious. As had been foreseen, the great alliance of gods and men tore itself apart. Myth and legend crumbled into Chaos. Darkness flooded the realms. Torture, slavery and fear replaced the glory that came before. Sigmar turned his back on the mortal kingdoms, disgusted by their fate. He fixed his gaze instead on the remains of the world he had lost long ago, brooding over its charred core, searching endlessly for a sign of hope. And then, in the dark heat of his rage, he caught a glimpse of something magnificent. He pictured a weapon born of the heavens. A beacon powerful enough to pierce the endless night. An army hewn from everything he had lost.

Sigmar set his artisans to work and for long ages they toiled, striving to harness the power of the stars. As Sigmar's great work neared completion, he turned back to the realms and saw that the dominion of Chaos was almost complete. The hour for vengeance had come. Finally, with lightning blazing across his brow, he stepped forth to unleash his creation.

The Age of Sigmar had begun.

CHAPTER ONE

FROM THE WORLD BEYOND

The chamber was vast, its vaulted ceiling lost in shadow. Its walls were smooth marble, black as night and dotted with false constellations of glinting silver. The chamber's floor was formed from irregular flagstones of blue and purple crystal that interlocked in a chaotic tangle. Dark doorways studded the chamber's walls, seemingly at random, while huge statues loomed menacingly along its edges. Sinister and avian beneath the stone robes that swathed them, these towering figures clutched burning braziers from which unclean firelight spilled.

At the foot of one of the strange statues, a figure stirred. A duardin Fyreslayer, clad in a dirt-stained loincloth and little else. The duardin's hair and beard were a deep, fiery red, matching the crest that rose from his battered helm. With a groan, the Fyreslayer opened his eyes. He breathed out slowly, muted sparks dancing upon his exhalation. Then he jerked suddenly, as though shocked.

The duardin pushed himself to his feet and cast around frantically. Spotting his axe and pick lying nearby, he snatched them up. Beyond the weapons was his pack, a threadbare satchel, clearly empty. He grasped it close all the same, clutching the meagre thing to his chest as though it were precious ur-gold.

With his belongings secured, the Fyreslayer closed his eyes, taking several deep breaths before opening them again. He dragged the fingers of one hand absently through his unkempt beard as he took in the statues, the crystalline floor, the distant ceiling hidden in shadow. Lastly the duardin inspected his own limbs and torso, eyes resting on the ur-gold runes that glimmered dully in his flesh.

'No,' he muttered to himself, the word coming out like the rustle of dead leaves. The duardin coughed, more sparks billowing forth as he cleared his bone-dry throat. 'No,' he rumbled again, voice louder now and tinged with something like anger, or panic, or both. 'This isn't... It's not...'

With a sudden cry, the Fyreslayer swung his axe, and forge-flame danced in its wake. He smote the base of the nearest statue, striking sparks and chips of stone from its taloned foot. With a hoarse roar, the duardin struck again and again, momentarily lost to the act of violence. On the fourth swing he stopped himself as suddenly as he had started, eyes widening and head darting left and right like a hunted animal.

'Fool,' he hissed at himself. 'Witless fool. Too much noise.'

The duardin's fears seemed borne out just moments later as, from a nearby entrance to the chamber, there came a low growl. Something bestial moved in the gloom, and keen, bird-like eyes glinted in the darkness. With a muttered curse, the Fyreslayer planted his feet and raised his axe in readiness.

'Well c'mon then,' he shouted into the darkness, 'come and get it over with. You'll not find Vargi Sornsson easy prey, you bird-faced bastards.'

There was movement in the darkened portal, and then a low,

lithe animal emerged. Sornsson's eyes widened as he took in the leopard-like body and proud, feathered head of an adolescent gryph-hound. The creature paced deliberately towards him, eyes locked on his. It emitted a low, warning growl as it came, clacking its beak menacingly. The Fyreslayer tensed, ready for the beast to pounce. Then another figure emerged from the doorway. Sornsson took in white and blue robes, a heavy warhammer, and dark skin, but his attention was still fixed on the animal that stalked him.

'Goldclaw!' called the newcomer in a deep, commanding voice. 'Away, girl. This is no creature of evil.' The gryph-hound bristled, then relented, circling protectively back to its master's side.

The Fyreslayer did not lower his axe, simply shifting his attention from hound to master.

'You're not, are you?' spoke the newcomer again, with a hard smile that didn't quite reach his eyes. 'A creature of evil, I mean. So you can lower those weapons.'

Sornsson shook his head, the gesture quick and jerky.

'Don't be so sure, stranger. Trust nothing in the tower. First appearances'll get you killed.'

'I have faith,' responded the robed newcomer. 'I am Masudro Yaleh. I am a warrior priest of Sigmar, and all I see is rendered clear in his light. Was there foulness in you, I would have seen it from the first.'

'Aye?' responded Sornsson. 'That's well and good, but how do I know *you* are what you say you are? I know I'm no servant of Tzeentch, but what of you?'

Masudro frowned thoughtfully, then held forth the small sigmarite hammer that hung on a cord around his neck.

'Were I a thing of evil, a creature of the Chaos God of change, could I wear this emblem, or let it touch my bare flesh?'

Sornsson spat.

'That could be as fake as the rest of your appearance. The tower… the tower cheats. It changes things. It lies.'

Masudro stared at Sornsson, gaze filled with concern.

'If that is so then there is truly no way I can convince you to trust me, and for that I am sorry. But that is the second time you have mentioned the tower, Vargi Sornsson. Of what tower do you speak? Where are we?'

For a moment longer, Sornsson stayed as still as graven stone, weapons raised and ready while his eyes searched Masudro's weathered features. Finally, as though he had come to some decision, the duardin let out a long sigh of exhaustion. His shoulders slumped, and he lowered his weapon.

'You truly don't know?' he asked, and Masudro frowned deeper at the resignation in the duardin's voice.

'Truly,' replied the warrior priest, 'but my suspicions are bleak.'

'Aye, and so they should be,' rumbled Sornsson. 'Welcome, Masudro Yaleh, to the accursed bloody halls of the Silver Tower.'

Man and duardin sat at the feet of the damaged statue, while Goldclaw pressed close to her master's side. Masudro's face was as grim as the sense of foreboding he felt. He absently rubbed his hammer amulet between finger and thumb as they spoke.

'So this is the tower of which the legends speak? The lair of the Gaunt Summoner?'

'It is,' replied Sornsson. 'And it's everything the legends claim and worse. A more evil place I've never seen, as twisted as the daemon that rules over it.'

The warrior priest nodded slowly. He looked at the duardin, sitting a few clear paces away, eyes watchful, weapons close to hand. Cautious as a hunted animal, thought Masudro.

'You have been here some time.' The priest's words were not a question.

'Aye,' said Sornsson, his eyes hollow. 'I'm a Doomseeker, of the Volturung Lodge. My oath brought me to the tower with… Well. They're gone now. It's just me.'

'So you came to this place on purpose?' pressed Masudro. 'You know how you got here?' For a moment the priest's hopes rose, but they were dashed again as the Doomseeker barked a grim laugh.

'I see where you're going with this. Forget it. The tower lets you in, but it doesn't let you out. It… moves. It changes. It cheats.'

The two were silent for a moment.

'And how long…?' began Masudro.

'A span of time,' interrupted Sornsson, suddenly angry. 'But what of you, priest of Sigmar? Eh? You ask a lot of questions, but you've told me precious little of yourself.'

Masudro raised his hands in a placating gesture.

'I am sorry, Vargi Sornsson. Truly. These are dire tidings, and in times of trouble I've a habit of looking to others' problems before my own.'

The Doomseeker said nothing, watching from under beetled red brows with one hand wrapped around the haft of his axe.

'I am a warrior priest of Sigmar, as I said,' continued Masudro, 'Goldclaw and I marched out of Azyrheim through the Clarion Realmgate. We accompanied an army bound for the siege of Darkenrift. We stepped through the realmgate and, instead of our staging area in the Sha'dena Valley, we found ourselves here. That was shortly before we met you. And honestly, that's all I know. How we came to be in this hellish place, I've no idea.'

Sornsson was quiet for a moment after Masudro's brief tale concluded, his expression unreadable. Then the Fyreslayer gave a grunt and pushed himself to his feet.

'Well, newfound companion, there's no point just sitting here forever. Eh?'

The warrior priest rose, and squared his shoulders.

'No indeed,' he responded, his resolve returning. 'I have a duty to the God-King. Goldclaw and I are needed at Darkenrift. Let us find a way out of this Tzeentchian prison, Doomseeker. But which way do we go?'

Sornsson scowled at each of the scattered entrances to the chamber. Masudro saw his new companion's eyes narrow in what looked like recognition, and gesture with his axe at an ornate bronze archway some distance to their left.

'That one looks familiar. I think,' said the Fyreslayer. Masudro nodded and, with Goldclaw prowling at their side, the priest and the duardin set off across the chamber.

At the companions' backs, a robed figure melted silently from the shadows and drifted slowly in their wake.

The companions passed beneath the archway and found themselves in a long corridor with a low ceiling. Their footfalls rang upon interlocking metal plates that described twisted, Tzeentchian shapes. From the crystalline walls stared myriad yellow eyes whose pupils followed them as they passed. Masudro recoiled at the sight. Sornsson merely ignored the staring orbs and pressed on up the slow slope of the passage. Goldclaw pecked angrily at the nearest eyes, eliciting disembodied squeals of pain until Masudro called her away.

'This place,' he called after Sornsson as he hurried to catch up, 'is it all so strange?'

'Hah, strange?' the Doomseeker shot back over one brawny shoulder. 'This is nothing.'

The corridor became a spiralling crystal stair that wound upwards for what felt to Masudro like hours. In places the walls became translucent crystal, through which the priest saw what looked like churning cogs and whirling stars. Finally, the stairway terminated in what seemed to be a dead end.

'Damnation,' exclaimed Masudro, feeling the press of claustrophobia for the first time. 'We shall have to turn back. All those stairs...'

'Wouldn't be so sure,' replied Sornsson. 'Look closer.'

Masudro stared at the wall where the corridor ended, reaching out a hand to touch its surface. He recoiled as the wall rippled like liquid silver. The priest looked to Sornsson for explanation. Ignoring his stare, the Fyreslayer stepped straight through the wall, disappearing into its flowing skin. Masudro felt a moment's panic at the thought of immersing himself in such obvious sorcery. Telling himself that he could not afford to be left behind by the only ally he had found in this place, the priest plunged through, pulling his balking gryph-hound with him.

For a split second, Masudro experienced a terrible sense of vertigo, and felt a bone-deep cold wash across his skin. Then he was stepping into a new chamber, bombarded instantly by strange sights and sounds. The warrior priest had time to gain an impression of creaking bookshelves and stone tables, all overflowing with scrolls and weighty tomes. Parchment carpeted the floor in thick drifts. It fluttered upon the walls like layers of tapestry, and even papered the ceiling high above. Every sheet of parchment was covered with lines upon lines of indecipherable scrawl that glowed blue as it flowed across pages or leapt spiralling into the air.

From ahead of him, between teetering bookshelves as tall as trees, came the flash and clangour of fighting. Without a second thought Masudro broke into a run, hammer at the ready and Goldclaw loping at his side. Slithering down a slope of parchment, the priest saw Sornsson ahead, locked in furious battle with several fearsome looking figures. The first was tall and heavily muscled, clad in barbarous finery and with a mohawk of raven-black hair rising from his scalp. Strange tattoos swirled across his bare flesh, and he wielded a huge longsword, with which he was parrying the Fyreslayer's furious blows.

The second figure was unmistakably a Stormcast Eternal, one of the God-King Sigmar's holy warriors. The sight of him made Masudro's heart leap. The armoured hero wore the silver livery of the Hallowed Knights Stormhost, and was using his tall shield to fend off the sorcerous blasts of a vile daemon of Tzeentch, his cloak billowing in the heat of each blazing impact. The thing was hideous, all rubbery pink limbs and leering, fang-filled maws, and as it capered back and forth between the stacks it flung bolts of kaleidoscopic fire into the fight.

'Silence in the library,' the daemon gibbered madly in a dozen voices, 'silencesilencesilence!'

Masudro skidded to a halt as he heard a sudden whisper next to his ear.

'The barbarian is not your enemy in this hour. Few are your allies in the tower. You must trust him.' The warrior priest looked around frantically for any sign of the speaker, but could see no one.

Now, though, he became aware that the Fyreslayer's opponent was not yelling war cries, but outraged curses. 'Back, you Khorne-cursed lunatic! Get back, or I swear on the Eightpoints I'll take your stunted head.'

Still Sornsson pressed his attack, ignoring the beset Stormcast and his daemonic foe as he sought to hack the barbarian limb from limb.

'Sornsson,' shouted Masudro, 'stop! The daemon is your enemy, not him.' The Fyreslayer shot a glance at Masudro, his expression incredulous.

'Are you mad, priest?' he shouted. 'He bears the marks of the Dark Gods.'

Masudro's mind reeled. The duardin was right, for the tattoos of the feral warrior were undeniably the runes of the Gods of Chaos. Yet he knew, just knew, that the barbarian was not their foe.

'Sigmar speaks to me,' Masudro shouted back. 'This is no servant of Tzeentch. He is a wanderer like us.'

At that moment, the barbarian, seeing an opening in the distracted Doomseeker's guard, kicked the duardin in the chest. Sornsson was sent reeling. Instead of pressing his attack, the dark-haired warrior spun and charged up the drifted parchments towards where the daemon leapt and capered.

Masudro watched as the barbarian wove around the Stormcast, using the bulky warrior and his scorched shield for cover until the last moment, then springing forth with the speed of a striking snake. His longsword lashed out, striking the daemon across its chest and ripping its unnatural body in two. Sulphurous flames leapt. Reeking smoke billowed. From the ruin of the unnatural entity, two smaller simulacra sprang, their hides blue and their single eyes glaring in sullen hatred.

The warrior priest now stepped forwards, ignoring the murderous glare of the still-winded Sornsson, and raised his amulet high. In a booming voice, Masudro spoke aloud the holy words of Sigmar. Cleansing light leapt, a holy brilliance that lanced out and struck one of the daemons square in the chest. The unclean thing howled in pain, its flesh boiling away to smoke and steam until nothing remained.

At the same moment, the Stormcast lunged forwards, dropping his guard and whipping his lightning-wreathed blade in a crackling arc. It struck the last of the daemons, which burst once again in two. Dancing yellow haemonculi leapt from its dissolving corpse, small things of flame and sulphur that shrieked angry curses.

'How many times must we kill these things?' cursed the

barbarian, as he and the Stormcast stamped and battered at the diminutive daemons. They crushed out the imps' fires one by one, recoiling from the scorching flames. They were joined by Sornsson, and quickly the three warriors extinguished the last of their unnatural foes.

In the lull that followed, Masudro watched the three warriors catch their breath. The warrior priest had spent decades keeping the peace in the shadowed quarters and cosmopolitan marketsprawls of outer Azyrheim. Always empathic, Masudro had become adept at seeing when common cause could be found between disparate peoples, and he saw that potential here. Then, quick as lightning, the Hallowed Knight's sword whipped up to point at the barbarian's throat, backing the dark haired warrior up against a tome-strewn stone table.

'We were not done talking,' grated the Stormcast from behind his helm's expressionless facemask. 'You still had to explain to me who you were, and why I should not slay you where you stood.'

Sornsson appeared at the Stormcast's shoulder.

'Just do him,' urged the duardin. 'Look at the tattoos on his chest. The talismans about his neck. This one's a slave of the Summoner, no mistake.'

Masudro started forwards, possessed once again by the sure knowledge that they could trust this barbarous figure. He stopped, conflicted. There was no denying that the warrior bore marks of devotion to the Dark Gods. So where did the compulsion to trust him come from? Sigmar? Or something else?

'I'm not your enemy,' growled the barbarian warrior, 'nor am I your friend. I'm Hathrek, Darkoath Chieftain of the Gadalhor, and my only duty is to my people.'

The Stormcast was unmoved, the point of his sword unwavering.

'So you said before the daemon attacked us, Hathrek of the Gadalhor. But do you deny that you worship the Dark Gods?'

'Of course I worship them,' spat Hathrek, 'but I'm no servant of the Summoner. I came here to bring that daemon to its knees. The same as the rest of you, yes? I had thought to walk my path alone. I don't have time to coddle the lovers of lesser gods.'

With lightning speed, the chieftain whipped his blade around, striking the Stormcast's weapon away from his throat. Throwing himself backwards, Hathrek rolled over the table and came up in a fighting crouch. The Stormcast and the Doomseeker went to follow him.

'Stop, you fools!' roared the Darkoath. 'We're surrounded by enemies beyond count, by dangers untold, and you want to fight me? The only damned Chaos worshipper to walk the halls of the tower who cares not about seeing you dead?'

'All servants of Chaos are my foes,' replied the Stormcast, advancing relentlessly around the table. 'Sigmar commanded that I defeat the master of the Silver Tower, and you bar my path. You are my enemy in the war eternal.'

'But I'm not barring your damned path,' snarled Hathrek in exasperation. 'And I'm not your enemy, though you're working fast to change that. I've never even seen a Stormcast Eternal before, nor a… a whatever the stuntling is.'

Sornsson growled angrily at this and his eyes flashed with furnace light.

'Don't worry, Chaos slave, I'll soon teach you to fear the Fyreslayers.'

The two warriors had now flanked Hathrek, who was backing slowly away on the balls of his feet, keeping both foes in sight and his guard up. Masudro could not help but notice that the chieftain's expression was less one of fear than sharp anticipation. This one was truly dangerous, he realised. And yet he'd rarely seen a servant of Chaos try to talk their way out of a fight before.

'Fine,' said Hathrek with forced lightness. 'Say I'm your enemy then. Say you insist on this fight. I have to win. I have to. The lives of my entire tribe depend upon it and I won't fail them. So I hope you're both ready to die, because I won't let you stop me.'

At this, the Stormcast paused.

'What lies are these? The champions of Chaos care not for protecting the lives of others. Explain yourself, swiftly.'

'Don't listen to him,' urged Sornsson, still edging forwards. 'Everything in the tower is lies. They flow through this place like lava through a forge.'

Masudro saw his opening and took it.

'Hold,' he said, his voice the commanding boom that afforded him such presence upon the battlefield. 'If we assume that all here is false, Sornsson, then we are lost. You and I should have killed each other on sight, were that true.'

'Still wondering why I didn't,' muttered the duardin, but he stopped his advance all the same.

'Hathrek, what lives do you speak of?' asked the priest. 'And do not try to deceive us, for I see with Sigmar's sight and I will know if you lie.'

'My tribe,' replied the chieftain, 'the Gadalhor. Several hundred souls residing in a walled village atop the Splintered Hills. For years now we've fought the Gor-kin and the orruks as they encroached upon our lands. We're losing. And so, through the wisdom of my village's shaman, I chose to walk the dark paths to this terrible place. I seek the power to protect my people. That's all.'

Masudro sensed unspoken desires behind the chieftain's words, but nothing he said seemed false.

'Noble intentions, perhaps,' said the Stormcast, 'but there is no true succour to be found in the promises of the Dark Gods. Had you turned to the light of Sigmar...'

'We tried,' snapped the chieftain, eyes flashing. 'In the early days we prayed to the heavens for salvation, and all we got was blood and sorrow. Your God-King could not help me, Stormcast, so I turned to those who could. Don't presume to judge me.'

'He speaks no lie,' said Masudro quietly, reading the pain in Hathrek's furious expression.

The Stormcast looked to the priest then, and with a slight nod, he lowered his blade.

'If it is as you say, then we have common cause. But I will watch you, Hathrek of the Gadalhor, and if you endanger my mission here I will strike you down with the fury of the heavens.' Sornsson shook his head in disgust, but stowed his axe and pick.

'Fine, I'm outnumbered 'n' I can't fight you all. But we'll regret trusting this one, mark my words,' he grumbled. Hathrek responded by sketching a mocking bow.

Ignoring his companion's displeasure, Masudro turned to the Stormcast.

'And what of you, my lord? What name should we know you by?'

'I am Avanius,' replied the Stormcast, 'a Knight-Questor of the Hallowed Knights. It is my honour to make your acquaintance, priest of Sigmar.'

'And mine yours,' replied Masudro, 'though I wish we had met under better circumstances.'

'Well,' interrupted Hathrek, blade still in hand, 'I'm delighted that we're not all planning to kill each other for the moment. Truly. But if that's the case, I need to move on from this place. I don't imagine the master of the Silver Tower will simply come to me.'

'You can seek the Summoner all you like, Chaos worshipper,' replied Sornsson sourly, 'I only wish to leave this hateful place for good and all.'

'Whatever we seek, Hathrek is right,' said Masudro. 'We won't find it here. So where do we go next?'

'We?' sneered the Darkoath. 'What we? I've no interest in letting the likes of you slow me down, or put a sword between my shoulder blades when you decide again that you cannot stomach the tainted company of a Chaos worshipper. I wish you whatever luck you deserve, but I fight alone.'

With that, the chieftain strode brashly up to the nearest door and wrenched it open. Masudro moved to stop him, but Sornsson grasped his arm.

'If you really want to ally yourself with this one, you need not chase him. I've seen this before.' Masudro frowned at the duardin as Hathrek vanished through the darkened portal, and it slammed shut behind him.

'He's gone,' exclaimed the priest after a moment, frustrated. 'Sornsson, what sense was there in such trickery?' The Fyreslayer crooked one eyebrow and scratched his ear.

'Just wait,' he muttered. 'Any moment.'

Behind them, the portal through which Masudro, Goldclaw and Sornsson had entered the library flared with light, before disgorging the Darkoath Chieftain. Hathrek pulled up short. An expression of surprise flashed across his features, followed by anger.

'What trickery is this? How...?'

'It's the tower,' interrupted Sornsson with grim certainty. 'This is what it does. It thrusts people together. Binds their fates. Whether they like it or no. At least 'til they stop breathing.'

'Troggoth dung!' exclaimed Hathrek. 'Lies!'

'Why would I lie?' Sornsson shot back. 'I'd be glad to see y'gone. Or dead. But we're not in a position to argue. You go back through that door, same thing's going to happen, and you're going to start looking like the fool you are.'

'Unless I kill you all,' snarled the Darkoath, brandishing his blade.

'Isn't that precisely what you were just arguing against?' asked Masudro. Hathrek drew breath to reply then stopped, defeated.

'How in the nether-realms do you know so much about it anyway, stuntling?' he demanded. Sornsson blinked, and cleared his throat.

'Been stuck here a while. Seen how the place works,' he replied. The others waited for more, but it seemed that was all the explanation the duardin was planning to offer.

'Well,' said Masudro, breaking the uncomfortable silence. 'I'll ask again then. Which way?'

They stood for a moment amongst the riffle and stir of the daemonic library, looking around at the handful of doorways and portals. None seemed more promising than the others. Then the Stormcast's helm twitched up as though he had heard some slight sound.

'That way,' he said, pointing to a heavy door of ironoak and purple crystal. 'I've a sense that what we seek is that way.'

Hathrek shrugged.

'It's as good as any other route for now,' he said, mockingly. 'If I must travel with you people then… lead on, oh great warrior of Sigmar.'

Avanius shot a look at the chieftain, before leading the way towards the doorway he had chosen, his cloak flowing behind him. The others hesitated for a moment, then followed the Knight-Questor, weapons in hand.

Once more a faded figure drifted in their wake, something diaphanous and ethereal. As he made to step last through the doorway, Masudro's head jerked round, his eyes searching the library intently. Yet there was nothing to see, for the figure had vanished the moment the priest turned his head. Frowning, Masudro stepped after his newfound companions and into the darkness beyond.

CHAPTER TWO

FIRE AND BLADES

The Silver Tower moved. It writhed and twisted. It changed by the moment. Complex beyond mortal comprehension, the tower's portals and corridors twined through time and space in a never-ending serpents' dance. Storms of raw magic raged through its chambers. Arcane machineries churned and hissed in the dark spaces between caged stars. Horrors of every twisted sort slunk through the tower's depths, or hunted its strange reaches in search of prey. The tower was like some vast spider's web, and the uneasy companions moved along its gossamer strands like wary flies.

'So what is it that makes you think you're leading us the right way?'

Avanius stopped at Hathrek's words, turning in the middle of the T-junction to face the rest of the group. Goldclaw trilled softly and cocked her head, as though seconding the Darkoath's question.

'I do not know,' replied the Knight-Questor honestly, feeling at a loss to explain himself. 'But more than once these last hours, when faced with a choice of paths, I have felt as though Sigmar has spoken to me, and told me the way.'

Hathrek cocked an eyebrow at this, looking around pointedly at the interlocked metal of the corridor in which they stood, and the crystal lights that spread their flickering illumination across it.

'Well then I hope that your God-King knows what he's talking about. I for one have absolutely no damned idea where we are.'

'Nor I,' agreed Masudro. 'But I trust in Sigmar's power. I wonder, though…' The priest glanced back, up the winding glass stairway they had just descended.

'What troubles you, Masudro?' asked Avanius, dismissing the Darkoath's barbed irreverence and following his companion's stare.

'I'll tell you what troubles me,' Hathrek cut in, 'I must have been in this tower for hours now, days maybe. Yet I've barely slept, and I feel next to no hunger. How is that?'

'Get used to it,' replied Sornsson gruffly. 'It's the tower. Stops you needing things like food and rest. Mostly, anyway.'

'You seem to know a lot about this place, duardin,' said Hathrek. 'One would be tempted to say too much. Perhaps you should lead us, if you already know the way?'

'What are you implying, Chaos slave?' growled Sornsson, hefting his axe.

'I think we're being followed,' blurted Masudro quickly. The others all turned to look at him, and Goldclaw growled protectively at their stares.

'Followed?' echoed Hathrek. 'By whom? Or what?'

'What makes you think this, Masudro?' asked Avanius, his voice earnest. The Stormcast was glad to hear his own suspicions aired by another.

'A sense. A presence. Several times, trailing at our backs

and watching... You say you've heard the voice of Sigmar, Knight-Questor. Well so have I – a whisper when we were in the library that told me to trust Hathrek.'

'A whispering voice?' said Sornsson, surprised. 'Like something speaking in your ear, or your mind? Y've heard it too?'

Masudro nodded, and the group stared at one another in alarm. Avanius nodded slowly.

'Really?' asked Hathrek after a moment. 'You're all following directions from an unknown whisperer, and yet I'm the tainted one? What made you fools think this was anything but Tzeentchian trickery? You of all people, stuntling. I didn't think you even trusted your own shadow.'

Avanius looked at the others, half angry, half confused. The Questor could see the same emotions upon the faces of his comrades.

'It didn't seem an evil thing,' replied Masudro eventually. 'I felt...'

'That I could trust it,' finished Avanius for him. 'That it was not of this place.'

'Oh, well, that decides it then,' spat Hathrek contemptuously. 'It must be some benevolent force for good that's sneaking after us through a daemon's lair, whispering in our ears. What else could it be?'

'Well,' replied Sornsson, not rising to the chieftain's bait, 'actually there is one other thing. The tower crawls with monsters and traps. I've fought more Tzeentch worshippers and dodged more stabbing spikes and fiery pits than I'd care to say since I came here...'

'And yet, aside from the daemon in the library, we have met only each other,' said Masudro, 'as though some benign agency guides our steps.'

The Fyreslayer nodded at this, but Hathrek chuckled sourly, his arms folded across his broad chest.

'*Hthrak'du*. Wishful thinking. You've all been deceived, and like a fool I've followed you this far. I'm doubtless further from the Summoner than ever. Enough. As I seem to be the only one the gods are defending from this bewitchment, I will lead the way from now on.' Hathrek turned towards the left-hand fork of the junction. 'I say we go this way. Follow me, or lose yourselves to the whispered path. I don't care.'

With a clatter of armour, Avanius blocked his path. The Stormcast understood Masudro's urgings for unity, but the scorn of one who had sold his soul to Chaos was hard to stomach. Moreover, Avanius felt little trust that the Darkoath would not lead them all into a trap, given half a chance. He held little concern for his own safety, for the energies of Sigmar flowed through his veins, but Avanius felt a duty to protect the priest and the duardin.

'You are not this group's leader, Chaos worshipper.'

Hathrek stepped close, his face inches from Avanius' sculpted mask. 'And you are, holy hero? Who named you our leader? Say Sigmar, and I'll run you through right now.'

Masudro stepped forwards, Goldclaw growling at his side.

'This is not helping. If we turn our blades upon each other, nobody wins.'

'I might,' smirked Hathrek, ignoring the look that Masudro gave him.

'I hate to agree with the Chaos worshipper,' sighed Sornsson, 'but he could be right. What if it is the tower, and he's the only one it can't touch? What if it's just leading us into a trap?'

'Exactly,' exclaimed Hathrek. 'Listen to the stuntling, not this great heap of ironwork and pious thoughts.'

'Enough!' barked Masudro. 'Antagonising one another is pointless. Hathrek, you believe you can lead us upon a better road? By all means try, and let us see what happens.'

Avanius shook his helmed head. 'This sits ill with me, priest.

I heard Sigmar's voice, I know it. But perhaps you are right. I will not find my way to the Summoner's lair through falling prey to manipulation and whispers.'

Reluctantly the Stormcast stepped aside. Flashing the armoured warrior a smirk, Hathrek pushed past him and strode down the corridor.

'Come then, my strange minions. Let me lead you on the path to glory. And if our whispering friend makes another appearance, we'll welcome them with steel.'

Mere minutes later, the group rounded a sharp corner and found themselves walking down a sloping corridor whose floor, walls and ceiling were made from flowing glass. Strange shapes rippled through their depths, the suggestion of screaming faces and lidless eyes. The corridor's end was lost in a haze of blue mists, while kaleidoscopic colours swam in the void beyond. Hathrek strode at the front of the group, his companions following warily behind him. Sornsson had drifted to the group's rear, and glanced over his shoulder every few moments.

'I've tried that,' Masudro told him wearily. 'Whatever's there, if anything is, it can hide itself from even my sight.'

'Aye, well, I'll trust duardin eyes over those of men,' responded Sornsson sourly. 'Meanwhile, what do you make of the Darkoath? You can't truly trust him?'

'I cannot, no,' replied Masudro quietly. 'I sense more to his being here than a selfless devotion to his tribe. And how does slaying the master of the tower save them anyway? From what legends I have heard, the Gaunt Summoner is a master of daemons, not orruks and beasts. No, there is plenty he's not telling us. But for now, he is an ally, and I believe that we must take those where we can find them.'

Sornsson snorted.

'Well, if it comes down to him or me...'

At that moment, Hathrek stopped suddenly with his head cocked to one side.

'Do you hear…?'

The others paused behind him. Goldclaw let out a trill, her feathered hackles rising. Masudro felt a shiver of dread premonition, like a ghostly breath upon the nape of his neck.

Suddenly, the Darkoath Chieftain broke into a run, dashing down the corridor as fast as he could.

'Move,' he yelled, a roaring jet of azure flame bursting from the floor where he had stood.

'Ancestors' oath!' cursed Sornsson. 'I knew we'd been too long without a bloody trap!' Giving Masudro a shove to get him moving, the Fyreslayer pursued Hathrek down the corridor at a frantic run. The others followed suit, crying out in shock as more jets of fire burst from the floor, walls and ceiling.

'Did we trip something?' yelled Masudro as he ran. 'Maybe tread on something?'

'Could be,' shouted Sornsson back over the bellow of flames. 'Or maybe the tower just knows.'

A blast of fire roared up beneath Avanius' feet, momentarily engulfing the Knight-Questor. Masudro knew a moment of horror before the Knight-Questor burst from the flames, his sigmarite plate scorched but unharmed.

The warrior priest was nearing the end of the corridor when Goldclaw slammed into his shins, making him stumble. The curse died half formed on his lips as blue flames spat out from the wall precisely where he would have been, and he thanked Sigmar for his companion's sharp instincts.

Ahead, the priest saw an octagonal doorway through which shone blinding light. He saw Hathrek plunge into its glare, Avanius following close behind with liquid flame still dribbling from his scorched armour. Fire leapt again, and Masudro heard

Sornsson curse in pain just before he lunged into the searing radiance of the doorway.

Avanius stumbled to a halt, feeling the heat slowly bleeding away through his armour. He thanked those who reforged him, noting that even his cloak had been no more than singed by the flames. Taking in the scene around him, however, the Hallowed Knight realised that they were not out of danger yet.

A forest of bladed brass pillars rose high into the air, whirling and spinning on all sides with a clatter of hidden cogs. The pillars jutted from the bronze floor of a huge metal pit, whose walls he estimated to be at least twenty feet high. Away between the dervish pillars and their deadly blades, Avanius spotted a set of curving stairs leading up out of this death trap. But there were more immediate concerns. Ringing the lip of the pit were shouting, jeering figures – humans, by the look of them, clad in the blue-and-yellow robes of Tzeentchian cultists. In the split second it took him to absorb these details, one of the cultists raised a twisted staff and fired a bolt of sorcery down into the pit. Ahead, Hathrek dodged nimbly aside, only to hiss a curse as one of the whistling blades nicked his bicep. The chieftain's blood spattered the pit's floor, and the watching figures cheered louder.

'Sigmar, grant me strength,' bellowed Avanius, ripping his blade from its scabbard as he barged past Hathrek and made for the stairs. This was a fight that only the chosen of Sigmar had the strength to win, he thought grimly. Magic blasts arced down towards him, and he raised his shield to ward them off. Sorcery met sigmarite in a rain of crackling sparks, and Avanius was driven to one knee as blast after blast rang from his shield. The Knight-Questor felt the unnatural fury of each impact, and prayed silently to his God-King for the strength to overcome it before his comrades were slain.

* * *

Masudro, Goldclaw and Sornsson had now made it into the bladed pit, eyes wide at the peril they found themselves in. The Doomseeker stumbled last into the chamber, the flesh of one arm scorched and squirming with mutation. Cursing, Sornsson gritted his teeth and dragged his axe blade like a rasp across the wound. The runes in his flesh glowed hot for a moment, as did the blade of his axe, and he cried out in pain as the corrupted skin sloughed away.

'I can heal you,' shouted Masudro, ducking a bolt of magic and narrowly avoiding taking a blade to the eye. 'But we've got to deal with the cultists first.'

The priest flinched as another robed figure pointed their glowing staff straight at him. For a second, the priest's perceptions slowed as the glowing orb of energy at the staff's tip seemed to swell until it filled his entire gaze. The next moment a heavy hatchet thunked into the cultist's chest, knocking him back out of sight.

'Thank me later,' called Hathrek, as he pulled another throwing axe from his belt ready to hurl. A bolt of sorcery arced down and exploded at his feet, throwing the chieftain onto his back.

'Avanius,' yelled Masudro, feeling the desperation of their predicament. 'We need your shield! We have to fight as one or we're going to get slaughtered!'

The Stormcast heard Masudro's shout. He looked back to where magic blasts were raining down around his companions, and knew where his duty lay. Wordlessly, Avanius turned back, lunging in front of Hathrek just as another salvo of blasts rained down upon the prone Darkoath. The bolts splashed against the Knight-Questor's shield, blackening its surface further.

'Get up,' Avanius commanded Hathrek. 'Stay behind me

and we'll make for the stairs. The others will die if we don't slay those cultists.'

For a moment, Avanius thought that Hathrek would spit some words of contempt, but a glance across the pit stopped him. The robed tormentors were toying with Masudro, Sornsson and Goldclaw, driving them back towards the bladed pillars with magic blasts.

'If they die, there's fewer of you to take a blade for me,' spat the chieftain, rolling to his feet and crouching in Avanius' bulky shadow. 'To the stairs, then.'

As the two warriors moved away in a crouching run across the floor of the pit, Masudro raised his amulet in an attempt to ward away the foul magic of the enemy. Bellowing prayers, he unmade the foul energies with sheer faith, first one then another arcane blast sputtering to nothing. But the priest could not maintain his shield for long, for his exhaustion grew with every blast he turned aside. He could see that blood was running freely from Sornsson's wounded arm, and the Fyreslayer was down on his knees, shaking and grey. Masudro glanced at Goldclaw, who was standing resolutely by his side, and felt a moment of sorrow that she too would surely die when he did.

'*You are not yet forsaken, holy warrior,*' came the whispering voice in his ear, making him jump with alarm. Masudro watched in amazement as a figure appeared amidst a whirl of smoke and flickering darkness, robes fluttering in an invisible gale. Lithe-limbed, it hung above the pit, faceless mask turned towards the cultists, shimmering staff lowered in their direction. Something was pulsing from the figure's stave, rippling, half-seen energies washing across the enemy. Masudro watched in astonishment at the effect they had. Tzeentch worshippers who had been taunting and chanting now turned upon one another with sacrificial blades drawn. They screamed and cursed, stabbing madly while others of their number tore at their own flesh with howls of abject terror. Masudro felt his gorge rise as one luckless figure plunged his fingers into his own eyes, gouging them out in squirts of blood while laughing madly.

Yelling in anger, the remaining cultists shifted their focus, and arcs of sorcerous flame converged upon the flickering apparition. As suddenly as she had appeared, the figure was gone, the magical flames exploding in a multicoloured fireball as they collided.

The whisperer had done enough, Masudro saw. Seizing their moment, Avanius and Hathrek had made it to the stairs. They pounded up them two at a time, Hathrek outpacing his erstwhile protector with a howl of bloodlust.

What followed was brutal and brief. The chieftain plunged into the nearest knot of cultists, hacking one almost in half with his longsword before doubling the next over with a knee to the guts, then staving in his skull with the blade's pommel. Avanius charged around the pit's edge and slammed, shield first, into another knot of foes. Bones broke. Bodies tumbled. Lightning arced from the Knight-Questor's sword as it sliced through flesh and muscle. Blood showered down into the pit, but Masudro ignored it. Leaving the last few Acolytes to his warrior companions, the priest steeled himself and laid his hands on Sornsson's scorched and mangled arm. A pale glow formed, like a new dawn. When it faded, the corrupted wound was healed with nothing but smooth scar tissue to show where it had been. Sornsson stared at the healed arm in amazement, the colour slowly returning to his face.

'I've never seen the like,' breathed the Doomseeker. 'Couldn't let it mutate... I've seen what the fires of this place do to... But... thank you.'

Masudro pulled the duardin to his feet, drained but at the

same time empowered by the miraculous energies that had poured through him.

'Thank Sigmar, not I. I'm just his vessel. Now come, I'd have some answers for what just happened.'

With Goldclaw prowling before them, Masudro and Sornsson wove between the still-spinning pillars and climbed the stairs. Above the fighting pit they found a broad chamber of bronze, gold and crystal, lit by leaping braziers that threw weird shadows up the walls. Hathrek and Avanius stood amidst the enemy dead, cleaning their blades and eyeing each other with something approaching respect.

'You fought well,' stated the Stormcast, inclining his head.

'I did,' agreed the chieftain with a wolfish grin, sliding his blade back into its scabbard and rolling his shoulders. The wound on his arm still bled a little, and with one finger he took some of the gore and daubed it across the skull-like rune tattooed on his chest.

Masudro chose to ignore the heathen gesture, and instead called out to the still air of the chamber.

'Another fought well to defend us here, also. We have seen you now, whisperer, and we would know who you are. Why do you follow us?'

'Aye,' agreed Sornsson, brandishing his axe. 'Show yourself. What do you want?'

The flames of the braziers leapt and crackled. Masudro's question hung on the air, unanswered. The companions waited.

CHAPTER THREE

TRUST AND BETRAYAL

Skrytchwhisker was lost. He still hadn't really admitted it to himself, though. His natural skaven pride wouldn't allow it. Instead, with no other ratmen around who could have put him in this predicament, the Clan Eshin Deathrunner had decided that it must be the fault of his Masterclan employers. Grey Seers, he thought scornfully. Always so convinced of their own cunning. Always so superior. Well those preening fools hadn't scry-seen how utterly labyrinthine the Silver Tower would prove, nor had they predicted its sheer scale. Skrytchwhisker had been sent to put a warpstone blade into the back of the Gaunt Summoner – he didn't know to what end, nor did he care. He only wished to see the job done, swift and deadly, and his reputation amongst the shadow-packs of Eshin increased accordingly. Instead here he was, squirming his way along a cramped brass pipe with absolutely no notion of whether he was getting closer to his quarry or further away. How long the assassin had been trapped amid the maze of the Silver Tower, he had no clue. Even with his finely attuned senses, Skrytchwhisker had soon lost track. But when he finally achieved his mission and returned to Blight City, he promised himself that he would make the puffed-up Grey Seers suffer.

The Deathrunner's ears pricked up at the sound of a voice, its warped echoes ringing strangely along the pipe. There was something up ahead, a vent or hole through which firelight flickered. The voice must have come from there. Hoping for some kind of lead on his target, or at the very least some unfortunate victim to vent his spite upon, Skrytchwhisker wriggled forwards on his belly until he could peer down into the chamber below. The skaven's beady red eyes widened at what he saw.

Unaware of their hidden observer, the companions waited with growing frustration. Hathrek drew breath to voice some barbed comment, when suddenly the braziers in the chamber flared. Their flames leapt high, then guttered out, leaving nothing but the muted glow of embers to throw scant illumination across the chamber. Sornsson cursed mightily. Hathrek hissed an oath in his dark and jagged tongue, feeling his battle-lust rise once more. Masudro raised his amulet and Avanius his blade, pale illumination spilling from both.

In that faint light, the companions watched with horror as the bodies of the slain foes began to twitch. As one, the fallen cultists' heads turned, fixing glassy eyes upon the companions. Nerveless jaws fell open, blood and shattered teeth spilling from them. From every dead throat came a croaking hiss.

'Greetings, champions,' hissed the dead men, voices raised in eerie unison. 'It is good that we speak at last.'

'What necromancy is this?' boomed Avanius, voice steady and untinged by fear. 'Who speaks?'

'It is I,' responded the dead men. 'The one you bade appear before you. The whisperer in the dark.'

'And are you some servant of the Great Necromancer, that you speak to us thusly?' asked the Stormcast.

As one, the half-seen corpses slowly shook their heads.

'Nooooo,' they moaned. '*Nagash holds no sway upon my soul. And I am no foe to you, champions. No fiend of the tower. I am an ally.*'

'If that's true, why this… puppet show?' spat Hathrek, searching the gloom in the hopes of spotting the illusionist. 'Why not appear in person?'

'*The very corpses through which you hear my words are reason enough for caution, think you not?*' responded the whisperer. '*Your blades are swift, your trust… comes somewhat slower. But you are the champions I seek. And I shall aid you.*'

The companions stared hard into the darkness, straining to catch sight of their supposed ally while watching the talking corpses for any sign of hostility.

'Who… what are you?' asked Masudro, one hand wrapped tightly around his hammer amulet. 'And why do you call us champions?'

Silence stretched long after this question. Hathrek noticed that Sornsson was motioning with his axe towards the chamber's nearest exit, trying to be subtle. The duardin raised his eyebrows in question, but the chieftain shook his head with a contemptuous sneer, and continued to peer into the darkness. Then the hissing voices came again.

'*In the interest of trust, I will tell you that I am a Mistweaver Saih, an agent not of evil but of Shadow. You may call me Eithweil.*'

'And why do you call us champions?' asked Hathrek, still poised in a loose fighting stance. In his culture, only those destined for greatness were given this title, and he felt trepidation and excitement in equal measure at the thought of the eyes of the Dark Gods sweeping closer.

'*It is spoken of in the legends of the tower,*' hissed the dead.

'*Champions will there be, seekers after the Summoner who shall set aside their enmities in search of their goal. They shall follow their guide to the lair of the daemon, and there put an end to his evils.*'

'Some of us couldn't give a spoil-scutt's nethers about finding the Summoner,' muttered Sornsson, drawing sharp looks from both Avanius and Hathrek. 'Some of us just want to leave this bloody place once and for all.'

'*Nonetheless,*' hissed the voices, '*you are the champions of legend, as have been those before you and those who will come after. Always it is thus.*'

'And you,' replied Avanius. 'I suppose you would style yourself as our guide? This is why you have whispered to us in the voices of those we trust? This is why you have steered our steps?'

'*Yes,*' hissed the dead, '*at least until the Chaos worshipper shunned my guidance and led you astray. Such it was that forced me to reveal myself, for you need my aid in person now. The true way is lost, and without me, so too will you be.*' Hathrek bridled at this, anger surging within him. This being was just another manipulative caster of bones. Her kind were always quick to blame a true warrior when their manipulations went astray.

'Hah! If we even believe that you are… whatever it is you say you are, and even if we believe you're on our side, how could you possibly know a way through this damned labyrinth? Unless you're a servant of the Summoner?'

'Or even the bloody Gaunt Summoner hisself,' growled Sornsson, cinders dancing around him as he scowled with anger and suspicion.

'*The cost in blood was high,*' murmured the dead, '*and the road of lies was long, but I was able to extract from a caged daemon the true path through the tower. Yet always this terrible place changes. Ever it warps and shifts. Step but once from the path, the entity warned me, and the route will be lost. The map becomes worthless.*'

'And by following Hathrek, you're saying we stepped from your route?' asked Masudro, brow furrowed. 'You ask us to take much on faith, and give us scant cause to trust you. Even if what you say is true, how then can you help us if we have lost our way?'

'*Trust begets trust...*' hissed the corpses, their heads thudding back to the floor one by one. Slowly the flames in the braziers crept back to life. As they did so the robed figure was revealed once more, standing lightly upon the lip of the pit. She held her staff across her body in both hands, and though her helm's facemask was a featureless blank, Hathrek saw wariness in her posture. Good, he thought spitefully. She should be wary of him.

'*...and so I choose to trust my true appearance to you,*' finished the Mistweaver, her voice seeming to echo from the air itself. '*There are other ways to find what you seek, if you will allow me to show you. I alone can guide you to the Gaunt Summoner.*'

The companions stared at this newcomer, and Hathrek saw hope and caution warring in their eyes. He decided to speak for them.

'Very well, Mistweaver,' he sneered. 'If you are what you claim, by all means lead on. I think it's clear we've no better way of finding our route, and wandering at random won't get us far. But one false move and I'll leave your head on a spike for the Blood Lord.'

'Only if I don't put my axe through her face first,' rumbled Sornsson menacingly.

'*I understand,*' replied the Mistweaver evenly. There was a flicker of light, and suddenly she was behind them, standing beside the archway to which Sornsson had motioned. '*Though I should warn you I am far from defenceless. You must earn my trust also, champions.*' Without waiting for a reaction, Eithweil turned and vanished through the archway into the shadows beyond.

The companions shared a frowning look, before following their strange new guide warily.

'Told ye it was this bloody door,' muttered Sornsson as they went.

Only once the chamber was empty did Skrytchwhisker drop down from the brass pipe high above. His tail twitched with excitement. The mage-thing knew the way to the Gaunt Summoner, and Skrytchwhisker had been cunning enough to track her down. Of course he had! All the Deathrunner had to do was get rid of the others and he would have her at his mercy. She would tell-speak her secrets soon enough. Skrytchwhisker prided himself on his skills of persuasion. Fangs bared with glee, the skaven scurried silently between the fallen bodies of the slain wizard-things and followed his new prey into the twisting tunnels of the tower.

The Mistweaver now led them along winding passages formed from crystal and clattering machineries. Masudro and his strange comrades climbed stairways of glass and gold that wound around fulcrum-pillars of living flame. He watched the newcomer for the slightest sign of duplicity. Goldclaw prowled close at his side, occasionally nudging his hand with her feathered head, as though to reassure her troubled master. Though the priest remained wary, the Mistweaver simply led them ever onwards. The Saih drifted above the ground, robes stirring as though tugged by the currents of some invisible ocean. Yet she moved with deceptive speed, and the others found themselves hurrying to keep up. In one dank and bone-strewn chamber the Saih conjured light from her staff, and Masudro saw foul things scuttling away into the fuming cracks that lined the walls. In another, she motioned for the companions to halt atop a glowing ziggurat. A procession of hunched, robed shadows shambled past its base, led by a diminutive figure with a half-moon head. Fiery clouds danced across the vast chamber's ceiling high above, their capricious light making the procession appear all the more grotesque and unsettling. The moment they were gone, the Mistweaver set off once more. She floated away down the ziggurat's steps, making for the swirling portal from which the hunched things had emerged. As the companions followed, Hathrek fell into step with Masudro.

'You claim to see the good in people, priest,' he began.

'Indeed, the good. The evil. The conflict.'

Hathrek favoured Masudro with a withering look. 'Spare me the sermon. You have your god, I have mine. Even Sornsson worships gold. This flimsy alliance depends upon us setting aside the fact of our differing faiths, so don't start undermining mine. I'm speaking of our new friend.'

'I know you are,' murmured Masudro, accepting that the chieftain would not hear his words. For now, at least. 'You want to know if I see duplicity in her.'

'I want to know if I should shove my sword through her neck,' replied Hathrek, so matter-of-factly that Masudro could not help a scandalised laugh. His mirth was stilled as Eithweil's whispering voice skirled around them.

'*I would prefer that you did not try,*' came the Mistweaver's voice. '*It would damage our fragile alliance.*'

Ahead, the diaphanous figure floated on as though nothing had occurred. Masudro and Hathrek shared a guilty look, then hurried wordlessly on.

Minutes later the companions had crossed the echoing chamber, and stood before the spinning energies of the portal. Hathrek looked to the Mistweaver, as did his strange comrades.

'*Here we find what we seek,*' came her voice upon the air.

'Beyond this portal lies one of the Gaunt Summoner's haunts, wherein the daemon may be compelled to appear.'

'As easy as that, eh?' asked Sornsson sceptically. 'You take charge, lead us down a few corridors, and suddenly we're at the heart o' the maze?'

'I tell you only what you will find beyond,' responded Eithweil. *'Make of that what you will.'*

'You say we will find the master of the tower beyond this portal?' said Masudro, 'Very well. If that is so, what must we do to escape this place?'

'We take his boon,' responded Hathrek savagely, feeling the rush of victory near at hand.

'We strike him down,' said Avanius at the same time.

'What I mean,' said Masudro into the uncomfortable silence that followed, 'is, what should we expect to face? Eithweil, you seem to know more than we.'

'There is a fane,' she responded. *'Within there is a statue. Only by its illumination can you find that which you seek.'*

'Good,' growled Hathrek, his dislike for the seer growing. 'Excellent. Prophecy as clear as the waters of the Clotted Sea. You can stand around and ask questions if you want. I choose action.'

Before another word could be spoken, the chieftain stepped determinedly into the portal.

'Alone, he will perish,' whispered Eithweil. Avanius and Sornsson shared a look, and Masudro sighed in exasperation.

'We need him,' said the priest simply, then stepped after the chieftain with Goldclaw at his side. Avanius followed, leaving Sornsson and the Mistweaver in the chamber. The duardin eyed the mysterious newcomer angrily.

'If you've led us false, I swear on my oath I'll kill you,' he rumbled.

'*Would you keep this one?*' came the sighing response, then Eithweil was gone through the portal, leaving the Fyreslayer gaping in her wake. His thoughts whirled, guilt and confusion tangling with resentment.

'She couldn't know,' he muttered angrily to himself. 'She bloody couldn't. How long's she been watching?' Hefting his weapons, Sornsson stepped after his companions. The duardin felt weightlessness, a whirling, tumbling sensation as though he were a mote in a gale. Lights and colours flashed past in a disorienting rush, then he was falling. Sornsson's warrior instincts kicked in and he rolled with the fall, coming to his feet unharmed. Instantly something was flinging itself at him, a snorting, bestial presence into which he buried his axe without conscious thought. Brackish blood splashed the Fyreslayer and, with a snarl, he kicked the corpse from his weapon. His attacker thumped to the floor, and he realised he had caved in the chest of a bird-headed Tzaangor. Sornsson spat steaming phlegm onto the avian creature and took in the madness around him.

The companions had landed in some kind of temple. The sense of scale was maddening, as though everything was somehow magnified. For a vertiginous moment, Sornsson felt he could reach out and touch the mosaic ceiling high above. Blue-tinged flagstones made up the floor, divided by metallic rails upon whose runners sat several bulky brass carriages bearing crystal prisms. The walls of the place were a dizzying patchwork of gold, silver and blue crystal, mixed together to confuse and nauseate. Dominating one end of the temple was a huge, spread-winged statue of a Lord of Change, the daemonic figure crafted from gold and leering down with lifelike malice.

All this Sornsson absorbed in a matter of moments, before focussing on his companions' plight. The floor of the temple swarmed with Tzaangors, the avian beastkin screeching and croaking as they attempted to surround the warriors. The twisted figures were a monstrous blend of human and bird-like beast, their muscular physiques strapped with random plates of golden armour and hung with weird tribal fetishes. The Tzaangors wielded a wild assortment of warped blades, and stabbed at the companions with their wickedly hooked beaks. Sornsson could see that every one of his allies was beset, barring the Mistweaver, whom he could not see at all. The duardin felt a moment of anger, then he was fighting for his life as more Tzaangors came at him. The runes in the Fyreslayer's flesh glowed as he stepped beneath the wild swing of a shrieking assailant and crunched his pick through its chest. Ripping the weapon free, he spun aside from the next lashing blade and hacked his axe through another Tzaangor's neck. As the beastkin's head thumped to the floor, Sornsson saw that his companions were faring well. Goldclaw was savaging one Tzaangor even as her master crushed the skull of another, while Hathrek and Avanius were carving their way through a press of reeling foes. The Fyreslayer saw shimmering motes of shadow flitting around the Tzaangors, and laughed as he understood.

'Not a traitor after all then, eh Mistweaver?' Sornsson could see they were winning, but there was no sign of the Gaunt Summoner.

As though his thoughts had conjured fresh danger, the air in the chamber crackled, and searing beams of light leapt from the eyes of the statue. The blinding energies struck the prisms, then leapt onwards to cut through everything in their path. Tzaangors shrieked as their flesh blackened and puffed to ash, and Avanius yelled in alarm as he threw himself prone beneath one of the leaping blasts. Turning upon their gimbals, the prisms swung wildly, sending roaring rivers of energy leaping out to blacken the walls.

'*The light,*' came Eithweil's voice in his ear. '*Turn it upon the statue.*'

Sornsson nodded and ran forwards, ducking under the obliterating glare of the nearest beam. He felt its heat wash across his skin, but he was duardin, of the Volturung, and he feared neither fire nor flame. Shoving a bloodied Tzaangor into the searing light, Sornsson ducked low and skidded to a stop next to one of the carriages. Throwing his shoulder against the mechanism, the Fyreslayer heaved, and the lens swung ponderously around.

'Mind the beam!' he yelled, 'Get the others!' Half blind, Sornsson could only hope that his comrades were following his lead as, crest singeing in the ferocious heat, he heaved the prism round to point directly at the statue.

Panting, Sornsson stepped back and saw with relief that the others had heard him, or else Eithweil had whispered to them too. The Tzaangors were dead or gone, and even as he watched, Avanius wrenched the last prism into alignment.

As it struck the towering statue, the light seemed to fracture into rivulets that spread and multiplied across the Lord of Change's form. Cracks grew in its shuddering metal skin, and with a sudden, titanic boom the statue exploded into fragments.

Sornsson was thrown back by the shockwave, hitting the floor with spinning chunks of brass raining around him. His ears rang with the force of the blast, the muffled whine slowly receding as the Doomseeker's hearing returned. As he sat up, Sornsson felt cold horror spread through him.

The statue was nought but a smouldering ruin, and from its carcass rose a terrible daemonic form. Flickering robes clung to a gangling, skeletal body. Three long, lithe limbs ended in taloned hands that clutched a dagger, a tome, and a crackling staff. Worst were the eyes, dozens of slitted yellow orbs that stared from the twisted horns of the daemon's silver helm.

Rising to his full height, the Gaunt Summoner bared needle fangs, and swept his arms wide in mocking invitation.

Sornsson felt panic grip him at the hideous sight. Here was the master of this terrible place, the architect of all his misery and shame. It had been too long. It was too much. Through a haze of panic, the Fyreslayer watched as Masudro, Hathrek and Avanius advanced upon their tormentor. The companions had gone just nine paces before the Summoner spoke, his voice the crackling of broken bone and shattered glass.

'Come to me. Take the power you desssserve. My boon is yoursssss.'

At those words, Hathrek quickened his pace, while Avanius faltered. The next moment, the Stormcast surged forwards and barred the Darkoath's path.

'You want his gift, not his death,' boomed the Questor, his voice accusatory.

'I've never said anything else,' Sornsson heard Hathrek spit. 'Now get out of my way.'

'I cannot,' intoned Avanius, raising his blade and shield. Hathrek snarled, and sparks flew as the two warriors' blades met.

The laughter of the Summoner was horrible to hear as Masudro and Goldclaw found themselves suddenly abandoned. Sornsson knew he should rise. He knew he must help. But it was all happening so slowly, and so fast.

Pink fire leapt from the Summoner's staff, engulfing the warrior priest and the gryph-hound in a polychromatic blaze. Holy light shone bright, driving the mutating flames back from Masudro's flesh. Goldclaw was not so fortunate, and the poor creature's shrieks of agony were terrible to hear as her flesh ran like wax and her bones exploded into powder.

Masudro howled at the fate of his companion, forging forwards through the stream of flames with his amulet held high.

At last, Sornsson was moving. But too slow. He would not be in time to help.

And then, as suddenly as he had appeared, the Summoner began to fade from sight.

'Not yet,' came his mocking voice. 'Not ready.'

Masudro stumbled to the statue's feet as the raging fires dissipated, and Sornsson saw the priest's eyes fix upon something on the ground, something that glinted where the Summoner had stood.

A loud clang echoed through the battle-scarred temple, the sound of Hathrek and Avanius' blades clashing again. Masudro wheeled towards them, his face a mask of fury. Sornsson saw a shape moving in the shadows behind the priest then. He raised a hand, shouted a warning. But too late. A wicked blade flashed in the gloom, tainted with glowing green poison, and Masudro was crumpling forwards, throat open from ear to ear. Sornsson caught sight of a beady red eye glinting in the gloom. Then the killer too was gone, vanishing in a cloud of sulphurous smoke, and Masudro's body was tumbling to the temple floor with blood jetting from his ruined throat.

CHAPTER FOUR

THE SHADOWED PATH

There was no way to bury Masudro's body. Instead, they burned him upon a pyre of fallen foes. Even Hathrek was quiet as the flames crackled and leapt, though outwardly he showed no contrition for letting the priest face the Summoner alone. Not so Avanius, who knelt before the burning body with his head bowed in prayer. A servant of Sigmar had died, and the Hallowed Knight owned part of the blame for that loss.

Sornsson stood off to one side, wreathed in gloom, his eyes distant as he puffed on his battered pipe. In his mind's eye, the Fyreslayer saw again the shadowy figure that had struck Masudro down. And he saw another thing, something that had come after, but that he did not yet fully understand. He pondered on that, and on what it might mean. For now, the duardin kept his own counsel.

At last, when Masudro was little more than ash, Eithweil shimmered into sight.

'*We must press on,*' came her voice, twining amidst the drifting embers. '*He would want us to keep going.*'

'You knew him not at all, and had no notion of his wishes,' came Avanius' flat voice as the Stormcast rose. His armour and shield bore fresh dents from where the Tzaangors – and Hathrek – had struck him, and lightning flickered across rents in the sigmarite.

'And I suppose you were his bosom companion?' asked Hathrek archly, nursing the gash on his forearm where Avanius had cut him. 'Knew all his deepest desires? Wants and needs?'

'I knew him little,' admitted the Knight-Questor, voice tinged with anger. 'But I know that he wanted for us not to give in, or allow our tormentor the satisfaction of seeing us beaten. He wished us to work together, to put aside our differences that we might emerge victorious. Even with his death, Masudro compelled us to lower our blades and stop fighting one another.'

It was the longest Sornsson had heard the Stormcast speak, and in the wake of his words there was an uncomfortable silence. It was the duardin who broke it, tapping out his pipe bowl and squaring his shoulders.

'Well then we should press on, unless you two are planning to start killing each other again?' he said, feeling nothing but weary resignation. 'Very long way to go. Maybe endless. We're barely over the threshold.'

'How would you know that?' asked Hathrek, narrowing his eyes. 'Have you seen this place before?'

'This, or places like it,' the duardin fired back over his shoulder as he made for the only visible exit. 'Come on, I'm fairly sure it's this way next.'

'How much do you know of this place, stuntling?' responded Hathrek, hurrying after the Fyreslayer. 'Exactly how long have you been here?'

'Too bloody long,' replied Sornsson, passing beneath the span of the crystal arch. With few other options, he knew the others would follow him into the gloom.

* * *

There came a time, that might have been minutes, or hours, or days later, when they found themselves in a corridor of looming golden sarcophagi. Seeking objects of use, the companions picked through the grave goods and glowing gewgaws piled around the standing coffins. As they did, they heard from within the slow tick and churn of clockwork. Worse were the occasional, muffled groans and thuds that all pretended not to hear while stuffing glowing phials into pouches, and testing the weight of glimmering magic blades. The strange sounds grew louder, more insistent. Finally, skin crawling, the companions hurried on into the azure mists.

Another time saw them step through a curtain of shimmering motes and onto a floating chunk of stone that hung in a dark and impossible void. Strange stars wheeled overhead with nauseating speed. More stepping stones stretched away in a winding path through the darkness. The companions were partway across that hungry void when daemons flowed from the ether, swooping down upon them on bladed wings. A perilous fight ensued, the champions leaping from one drifting stone to the next and driving off the unnatural void-beasts with blade and spell. More than once the creatures' fangs bit home, and by the time the companions plunged through a whirling portal to escape, all were bleeding from vicious bites.

Another moment saw a lull, a pause in a chamber of dripping pipes and tinkling, broken fountains, where they caught their breath and bound their wounds.

'What happened before–' began Avanius, his troubled conscience compelling him to speak.

'You want to kill the Gaunt Summoner, and waste the one chance I have to seize the power to save my tribe,' interrupted Hathrek. 'Because you are short-sighted and pious where you could be strong.' The bitterness in the chieftain's voice was tangible.

When Avanius replied it was not with anger. 'My liege, the God-King Sigmar, gave orders that I come here and defeat the master of the Silver Tower. Those were the exact words.'

'So you just obey,' sneered Hathrek, 'like an eager hound?'

Avanius nodded, finding that his desire to honour Masudro's death had dispelled the righteous repugnance he had first felt towards Hathrek. Matters of allegiance and duty were more complex in this place. He understood that now. Avanius did not want to pick a fight with the Chaos worshipper, strange as that seemed even to him. He only wished to make this teetering soul understand.

'I obey, for it is my sworn duty. It is my oath. I fight for a greater cause, using selflessly the might that Sigmar gave me, rather than turning it to personal gain. That is my strength, Hathrek.'

'We both want to save people, Stormcast,' said Hathrek distantly, watching water drip into a nearby pool. 'The difference is, I know those I fight for. You think you can save everyone. Thus you are deceived.'

'No,' replied Avanius. 'It is you who is deceived. By yourself. Perhaps you are here for your people. But you follow a dark and dangerous path, with no guarantee of success and no knowing how long the road will be. If helping your people was all you desired, you would have stayed with them. Part of you wants this.'

Hathrek pushed himself angrily to his feet, reaching for the pommel of his sword before snatching his hand away again.

'When we next see the Summoner, I will do what I must,' he spat, and stalked away.

'So will I,' said Avanius, his voice still sorrowful.

* * *

After, or perhaps before, came another time when the only way forwards was through the noxious gullet of some huge and horrible beast. Reeking vapours hung thick around the companions, and they cursed and choked as sizzling acids burnt their skin and gear. After Sornsson wrenched him from amid the peristaltic contraction of the thing's guts, Hathrek looked at the duardin with exhausted frustration.

'How much longer can this go on?' gasped the Darkoath, warring with his feelings. The duardin snorted gruffly and turned away.

'I told you before. For all I know it's never-ending. Come on.'

With that, Sornsson struggled onwards, leaving Hathrek to face the blank scrutiny of Eithweil.

'It is not endless,' came her whispering voice, and the chieftain was quite sure that at that moment she spoke only to him. *'The duardin will not say so, but he knows this road. Its steps are familiar to his feet. And we are going the right way.'*

On and on it went, until time lost all meaning and the urge to keep moving became an end in itself. The only alternative was to collapse in defeat, and none of the companions was willing to do so. They knew little hunger or thirst, though they were sure they should have starved long before. The runes still glowed dully in the Fyreslayer's scarred flesh, though they surely should have burned out by now. There was no logic to any of it anymore, but they pressed on regardless. They would not let the Gaunt Summoner win.

It would have shocked them to know that the daemon they sought was following their trials with interest. In fact, as the daemonic sorcerer hunched spider-like over the mirror in which he watched them, he crooned with pleasure each time they emerged victorious from another test or trap. When the Mistweaver indicated pressure plates before they could be trodden on, the Summoner smiled his shark's grin. The Mistweaver must always see clearly, even as she deceives, he thought indulgently. When the Darkoath Chieftain and the Stormcast stood back to back, their blades forming a whirling wall that drove off a tide of shrieking Scuttlings, the Summoner applauded delicately. When the group crossed a crystal chamber in which bones and rags were strewn, the Summoner watched the Fyreslayer stop and furtively slip the ring from the finger of one of the skeletons, sliding it onto a digit of his own left hand. The duardin hastened on, pale and shaking, and the Summoner chuckled with malicious glee, waving one finger chidingly at the fading image. The Doomseeker, he thought. So volatile. So strong, and yet so brittle. Occasionally the daemon moved away from his mirror. He stalked around his sanctum, spinning dangling cages that contained shrieking birds, poring over ancient tomes or absent-mindedly mixing strange potions in crystal philtres. Yet always he returned to scrutinising the champions as they navigated his maze. Always his many eyes – each plucked from a different, screaming victim – watched with fascination as the strands of fate flowing before and behind the champions changed in hue and texture. In particular, his eyes lingered long on the Darkoath Chieftain. As his strand of fate stuttered between glinting gold and cloying black, the daemon licked cracked lips with a squirming tongue, and crooned to himself once more.

Elsewhere, trailing the companions like a shadow, Skrytchwhisker muttered and cursed. The assassin did not struggle to keep pace with such plodding beings, but the ever-changing nature of the tower compelled him to stay closer to his quarry than he liked. Too far back, and he was worried that the path might shift, spiriting them away forever. More than once, the skaven just barely managed to dive into some shadow or cover in time to avoid being spotted by one of the whiskerless fools.

It would not do to underestimate them though. Oh no. Skrytchwhisker had not gather-seen just how strong or dangerous they were at first. Only when he took the priest did the Deathrunner fully grasp what a potent band of warriors he faced. The proof was there not just in their weapons, their magic, and their obvious warrior skill. It was the way they had betrayed one of their number so callously, two of them engaging in an open leadership challenge even before his corpse had hit the floor. To engineer their leader's death and be brazenly fighting for dominance before he had even finished dying? Skrytchwhisker would have been impressed, if he hadn't been so unnerved.

Thus the assassin had decided to change his strategy. No longer convinced that even he could defeat them all without an element of personal risk, the skaven resolved to follow the group, and to let them lead him to his true victim. He might even aid them, if the chance arose. But he would stand over all of their corpses in the end. Skrytchwhisker scurried on. Soon-quick, his genius plan would bear fruit. He was sure.

The group had wandered out of time and beyond sanity, through mists of forgetfulness and voids of aching loss. They followed the directions of Vargi Sornsson, who continued to claim that he knew their route, though he would not tell them how. Avanius pressed the duardin until he realised that, short of drawing a blade, he would not compel the stubborn Fyreslayer to speak. Even then, he doubted it would have worked. So they trudged on, wounded, battered, exhausted without need for sleep, until at last they descended a winding tunnel of stone that became ever more rough and natural-looking as they progressed. Sornsson, tramping relentlessly at the head of the group, rounded a corner and stopped short.

'Mushrooms!' he exclaimed. As Avanius caught up he saw that the darkness ahead was lit by hundreds of glowing lights, each one a rubbery-looking fungus sprouting from the walls, ceiling or floor. Some were no larger than a man's thumb, while others were great bloated things, bigger than a troggoth and looking fit to burst.

Further down the tunnel's throat, the luminescence grew brighter. Thrown around another corner by the strange light, distorted shadows cavorted and danced. Still distant, Avanius could hear shrieks and whoops, screams and gibbering, all set to the arrhythmic thumping of drums.

'Sounds like a ritual,' commented the Knight-Questor quietly, unsheathing his sword.

'Sounds like another bunch of fools for us to kill,' grinned Hathrek.

'Agreed,' nodded Sornsson. Eithweil simply drifted nearby, shimmering on the edge of visibility.

'Hathrek, you lead,' said Avanius, 'Sornsson and I will follow you in, to keep them from flanking. Eithweil…'

'I will hang back, and work such terrors upon their minds that the death you bring will seem sweet release.'

'I could not have found better words, witch,' smirked Hathrek. He unsheathed his long blade from its back-scabbard and began to pick his way between the quivering mushrooms. The others followed, Eithweil vanishing from sight amid the gloom.

As they got closer to the bend in the tunnel, so the pounding of drums became louder, and the riotous screeching of the revellers more frantic. Amongst those awful voices Avanius could discern a deeper rumble. Hathrek glanced back at him and mouthed 'something big'. The savage delight in the chieftain's eyes caused the Stormcast to shake his head despairingly.

The next moment, they were round the corner, and Hathrek howled a sudden battle cry. He launched himself forwards, charging full tilt down the tunnel, and Avanius led the rush to keep up. The champions burst into a wide, low-ceilinged cave whose corners were crammed with obscene masses of glowing mushrooms. Emerald light spilled from a huge mystic symbol engraved into the dirt floor, and in that weird illumination the dark revel turned as one. Cultists and Tzaangors, many daubed with weird, glowing symbols, cried in outrage and reached for jagged blades. Yet Hathrek was already amongst them, swinging his sword like some lunatic woodsman.

As the chieftain drove into his foes, the Questor and the Doomseeker fanned out to either side. They formed a lethal battle-line, hemming their more numerous enemies in and giving them no chance to react. Avanius smashed his shield into the face of a charging cultist, shattering the man's skull, then stabbed his lightning-wreathed blade into a Tzaangor's shoulder and ripped it free in a spray of blood. In his peripheral vision, Sornsson was a whirling dervish. Axe and pick whipped round and round in vicious arcs, leaving trails of blood in their wake. Angrily, the revellers pressed forwards, shrieking curses and brandishing blades. Avanius saw one stab a knife into Sornsson's thigh, while another sank his teeth into Hathrek's neck, only to have his own throat ripped out for his troubles. Then the Saih unleashed her powers. One by one, the dark revellers turned upon each other, ran headlong into rock walls, or stabbed their daggers into their own eyes and throats.

Avanius began to think that their surprise attack would carry the fight with ease, but then a huge, dark shape pushed forwards through the throng. Iron-hard muscles rippled beneath taut, sigil-covered flesh. The thing was humanoid in shape, but monstrous, over twice the size of Hathrek. A long tail whipped in anger, while red eyes glowed like coals. Arcing horns spread like a crown from the massive beast's head, and an elaborately carved staff glowed with magical power in one fist. As it chanted mangled words in some dark tongue, Avanius realised that this thing was far more dangerous than any of the chattering fiends around it.

With a snort, the huge beast smashed one of its own throng aside with its heavy staff, then levelled a blast of sorcery at Avanius. Blinding light exploded as the Stormcast raised his shield, only to have it torn from his grip by the force of the impact. Bone cracked, pain roared like fire up Avanius' arm and into his shoulder, and the Knight-Questor slammed back against the chamber wall.

Blowing steam from its nostrils, the huge beast-wizard turned and grunted a series of harsh syllables. Through a haze of his own agony, Avanius heard a pained cry that seemed to echo from everywhere at once. Suddenly the Mistweaver flickered into view, slumped on her knees in the mouth of the tunnel. Blood spattered the ground beneath her.

'Ho there,' shouted Hathrek, 'beast! Come fight someone worthy!' The monster raised its staff again, but Hathrek was ready. As the roaring blast leapt forth, Avanius saw the Darkoath throw himself out of the way, allowing the beam to pass over him and explode against the cavern wall. The hulking beast stomped closer, leering down at the prone barbarian. It paused as Hathrek grinned back.

Avanius watched as Sornsson hit the thing like a cannonball, slamming into his enemy while Hathrek had it distracted. The duardin buried his pick in the Ogroid's back, then hacked his axe between its shoulder blades for good measure. Wrenching both weapons out, the Fyreslayer jumped away as the monster turned and lumbered after him. The next moment it roared in pain as Hathrek's sword point burst from its chest. Glowing blue blood spurted. The beast crashed to its knees, mouth working as it tried to voice some last curse or incantation. Dismissing the pain of his injuries, Avanius pushed himself away from the cavern wall and crossed the gap in three swift paces. His blade whipped out in a crackling arc, and the Hallowed Knight lopped the beast's head from its shoulders.

As the creature's headless body toppled sideways, Hathrek laughed and Avanius limped away to retrieve his shield. The beast-wizard had been the last living foe in the chamber, and the fight appeared over. Yet Sornsson waited, tense, until he saw the shadows flicker. Giving a sudden shout, he lashed out with the butt of his axe and caught the half-seen shape bent over the monster's corpse. Eithweil cried out as she was knocked to the floor, her voice coming, for once, from behind her mask. In her hand was clutched a glinting fragment of something, a jewelled golden segment on a heavy chain.

Avanius and Hathrek stood and stared as Sornsson stood over the revealed Mistweaver.

'That's the second time you've done that, Eithweil,' the duardin growled, his anger simmering close to the surface. 'Care to explain?'

'Second? Done what?' Hathrek sounded confused.

'Aye,' rumbled Sornsson. 'She did the same in the temple. Right after Masudro... When the Summoner vanished he left something behind. Something the priest saw. Something she pocketed while you two *jak'nachs* were still battering each other.'

'You are only telling us this now?' asked Avanius sternly.

'Wanted to be sure,' replied Sornsson, his pick hanging menacingly above Eithweil. 'Didn't like the idea she was lying to us.' He had come to mistrust the evidence of his own senses since becoming trapped in the tower's embrace, but this was something else.

'*There was no lie,*' the Mistweaver spoke from the air once more, voice frosty and menacing. '*I simply did not tell you about the amulet.*'

'What amulet?' Hathrek's voice was dangerously low.

'*Vargi Sornsson,*' came Eithweil's voice, ignoring the question, '*you will lower your weapons and step away from me or I shall make you peel the skin from your own bones.*' The Fyreslayer gritted his teeth and stood his ground, though he didn't doubt for a moment that she could make good on her threats. In the tower, he had found that no truth was bought without pain.

'What amulet?' repeated Hathrek, voice rising in anger. Avanius stepped forwards. He knelt down and offered a hand to the Mistweaver. She ignored it, blinking out of sight. Avanius straightened, and Sornsson saw angry lightnings flickering in the eyes of his mask.

'If you know something and are not telling us,' the Knight-Questor said to the air, 'if you are endangering us or playing us false, all the tricks and illusions in the realms will not aid you. And remember that even should you kill me, I will come back for you.'

'What. Amulet?' asked Hathrek again, his tone exasperated. For a moment, Sornsson was sure that Eithweil still would not speak. Then came her voice, a cold zephyr of sound.

'*I did not tell you until now, because I did not know if I could trust you.*' She ignored Hathrek's incredulous snort. '*I retrieved more from the daemon than just the map. I learned also of the amulet. I learned how to listen for its song, how to hear it no matter how distant, and follow that sense to each fragment in turn.*'

'So when you led us to the Summoner's lair in the temple…' began Avanius, shaking his head.

'*I did not lead you to the Summoner, but to a fragment of the amulet that, if whole, can be used to conjure him,*' finished Eithweil.

'So this amulet brings us to the Gaunt Summoner?' asked Hathrek angrily. 'How many pieces are there? Why in the Dark Brothers' name did you let us think we were just wandering lost after some half-mad duardin?'

'The duardin knows the way,' answered Eithweil, her voice whipping around them like an autumn wind, and Sornsson felt a pang of alarm. '*It is fragmented, veiled in the mists of timeless misery. But he knows. He has seen this all before. What of the ring, Vargi Sornsson?*'

Now it was the Fyreslayer's turn to face the scrutiny of his companions. He stared back stubbornly, but could not hide the twitch beneath one eye, or the ornate silver ring they now noticed on one hand. Even here, thought the Fyreslayer resignedly, you could only hide your shame for so long. Sooner or later, someone always smelt the rot.

'Aye,' he said, as though dragging the words up from a deep well, 'I've been here a long while. A terribly long time.'

'And what is the ring she speaks of?' asked Avanius.

'When I first came here it was as a bodyguard,' muttered the Fyreslayer, shame knotting his guts into a bitter ball. 'A scholar. A human from Azyrheim. He sought the secrets of the tower and, for a sum of ur-gold, I oathed myself to his protection.'

'Then where is he now, stuntling?' asked Hathrek.

'Dead. Bones, back along our path,' replied Sornsson. In his voice there was a terrible depth of exhaustion, yet it was as the tip of a frostberg to the vast despair that lurked below. 'They came upon us at camp. Too many. I tried. I... Well, he died, and my oath was broken. So I tried to find my way out. But it's always the same. New people come. New faces. They try. They fall. Then I'm alone again, because the tower never lets you go. The ring was his, meant to be lucky. Thought it might bring me some at last.'

'*How many champions have you fought alongside, Doomseeker?*' Eithweil's question was barely more than a whisper, but Sornsson's eyes snapped back to angry focus at the words. His shame burned up like mine-gas before a naked torch, igniting into flames of rage that danced around him.

'Lots, not that it's your business, shadow witch! And my secrets don't excuse yours. What else aren't you telling us? Eh?'

'*There is nothing more,*' replied Eithweil after a moment. '*We simply need to overcome the trials of the tower, and claim the amulet fragments. I can sense their magic call, and guide you to them. But I cannot claim the fragments alone.*'

'And hence you need us,' said Hathrek sourly. 'What do you care about facing the Gaunt Summoner anyway, witch? Do you seek his boon, or his death?'

'*Neither,*' came the response, the words seeming to come from behind, and then ahead. '*I seek to change the fate of distant things, and events that have not yet come to be. More than that you need not know, but that your success will spell my own, one way or another.*'

For a long moment, the companions looked warily at one another.

'What choice do we have?' asked Hathrek. 'Do either of you know the way?' Avanius shook his head, and Sornsson spat.

'Not one that leads to aught but death and loneliness,' growled the duardin.

'Then we need her,' asserted Hathrek. 'I have to believe that we can reach the Summoner. That we can win. But if this is falsehood, witch...' He raised his voice to the air.

'*Always, threats,*' came the Mistweaver's response. '*You have made plenty of those, Hathrek of the Gadalhor. So many that I wonder at their veracity.*' She shimmered back into view at the far edge of the cave, the glow from her staff illuminating a narrow passage hidden amidst a cleft in the rock. '*But whether you mean me harm or no, it is a risk I must take. Matters of grave import hang in a balance you could not comprehend, and I will do what I must. Trust me, or rot here. Come.*'

With that, Eithweil led the way from the cavern and into the darkness once more. Sornsson looked to each of his companions in turn, and saw that they meant to follow her, despite her duplicity. The duardin was surprised to find that he did too. Though it was clearer than ever that none of the champions were precisely who they claimed, the revelation of the amulet filled him with a sense of purpose he had long been without. It would do, he thought. For now.

CHAPTER FIVE

THE EMPTY HEAVENS

It might have been mere hours later, or perhaps it was years, when, amidst the silent gloom of a vast gallery, a mirror's surface blossomed with violet fire. Glass seethed and bubbled, running like tallow. It began to churn, as though stirred with an invisible ladle. Faster and faster the liquid glass spun, purple energies billowing from it in clouds. The next moment, the companions spilled from the surface of the strange portal, tumbling across the dusty floor of the chamber. One by one they rose to their feet, casting wary glances back at the mirror that still spun like a whirlpool behind them.

'Well,' said Hathrek, 'that was unpleasant. I'm still not sure even an amulet fragment was worth being immersed in that much filth, but at least the blood washed it off, eh? Now where are we?' He watched as Eithweil raised her staff, and glimmering silver light spilled from its tip. A huge, dusty chamber was revealed, galleries stretching away above. Sornsson cried out and raised his blades as spread-winged skeletal horrors leapt into view.

'Steady, friend,' said Avanius, a slight smile in his voice.

'Those can't hurt us.' Sornsson lowered his weapons, coughing in embarrassment as he realised the skeletons dangled from the high ceiling on wires like strange museum pieces.

'Can't be too careful,' the duardin muttered. 'I recall y'said the same thing about that glass statue that almost lopped off your head.'

'True, he did,' smirked Hathrek, privately glad that the duardin had reacted to the hanging beasts before him. 'But all the same, try not to soil your loincloth, stuntling. The gods know when you might find another…'

'Eithweil, what is the count?' asked Avanius, evidently keen to head off another altercation between man and duardin. Hathrek shook his head; this conversation had become ritual for the Stormcast and the Saih, ever since they had recovered the third fragment from within the geared workings of a huge, mechanical gargant. The Mistweaver drifted high above them, robes flowing amid the shadows as she inspected one of the dangling, draconine skeletons.

'Seven. We have seven fragments of the amulet now, Avanius. As well you know. But I feel the eighth. It sings to me. It is near.'

'Then let's not drag our heels,' said Hathrek. 'It feels like we've been wandering this place for a thousand years.'

'Don't even joke,' snapped Sornsson.

'Very well, we move,' said Avanius. 'Eithweil?' The Saih faded like a dream, only to appear some distance away across the dusty flagstones.

'Follow,' came her voice in their ears. Steeling himself for the next ordeal, Hathrek led the way, tracking weary footprints through great drifts of dust that had not been disturbed for time unguessed.

At the companions' backs, one more dark figure sprang from the surface of the swirling mirror and scurried into the shadows.

* * *

'No,' said Avanius, aghast. 'No, this cannot be.' The Stormcast stood in the flickering light of golden torches, feeling a mix of bewilderment and horror as he stared at the two huge statues before him. The statues stared lifelessly back from masks that mirrored his own, golden swords and shields clutched in their huge golden hands. Each of the Stormcast effigies stood at least forty feet tall, and dozens of lit torches flickered in sconces set about their torsos, shoulders and limbs. Between them, beneath a beautifully frescoed ceiling of angelic figures and glimmering stars, brass steps inscribed with Azyrite runes led up to a huge golden portal. Tzaangor bones and tattered cultist robes lay scattered upon the steps as though the Tzeentch-worshippers had been slain trying to pass through. Again his mind rebelled at the thought – all of the gates to the Heavens were sealed tight, save those the God-King had opened for his war against Chaos. There could be no such entrance here. Through the portal's surface a marble floored gallery was dimly visible, its walls hung with beautiful tapestries and lit by brilliant sunlight that poured through some unseen window.

'Is that daylight?' asked Hathrek. 'Real daylight?' The longing in his voice was palpable, but he stayed where he was.

'It is Sigmaron,' replied Avanius. 'And yet it cannot be. The God-King would not permit a portal into this nether-realm to breach the Heavens. This must be a trick.'

'I can tell you only that the song of the amulet drifts from beyond that portal,' came Eithweil's voice. *'As for the rest, I know not.'*

Sornsson had been silent thus far, staring at the portal with wide eyes. Now he started forwards.

'Wait,' cried Hathrek, 'I'm not going through there. Sigmaron? I'd sooner dive into a nest of vipers!'

But Sornsson was jogging up the bronze steps now.

'I've never seen this place,' he shouted back at them. 'It's a way out. It's a bloody way out!'

'No,' called Avanius, starting up the steps after the duardin as he realised what his comrade intended. 'There's something wrong here. Sornsson, wait.'

But there was no stopping the Fyreslayer. He was running now, up the steps as fast as he could go. The others rushed behind him, but too slowly. With a wild cry, Vargi Sornsson plunged into the golden portal, and its energies leapt outwards in a roaring tide. Golden tendrils whipped and lashed, winding around the companions with incredible strength. Even Eithweil was plucked from the air, suddenly visible as the glowing tentacles grasped her. Yelling and fighting, the companions were borne helplessly up the steps, and plunged through the golden portal.

Hathrek pushed himself to his feet, skin still tingling where the golden energy had grasped him. The Darkoath Chieftain squinted against the sunlight, dazzling after so long surrounded by gloom. The light felt warm upon his bare skin, sinking through his flesh in a way that was almost healing. Then he remembered where he was, and cursed as he looked wildly about for foes.

Nearby, Avanius and Eithweil were also finding their feet upon the marble floor. Sornsson was nowhere to be seen.

Avanius shook his head as though clearing his thoughts, then looked about him in wonder.

'Sigmaron. The city of the God-King himself. It is. But how can this be?' He looked back, taking in the shimmering golden portal filling the passageway behind him. Beyond, the interior of the Silver Tower could dimly be seen. 'I do not recognise this corridor, but there is no way that this portal could be here, or anywhere in this place.'

Eithweil drifted down the corridor. Hathrek watched her flicker in and out of sight as she crossed the golden sunbeams falling from high arched windows off to their right.

'We must find Sornsson,' came her whisper. *'He may be in peril.'*

Swiftly, the three of them hurried along the corridor. Hathrek's eyes darted like those of a hunted animal, and he kept his blade ready in his hands. Panic tightened his chest, and his heart thumped in his throat.

'If this is Sigmaron,' he said urgently, 'Avanius, you know I will have to fight.'

'If it truly is,' replied the Stormcast, 'then I will speak for you.' Hathrek looked at the Knight-Questor in surprise, but Avanius' mask gave nothing away.

The companions reached the end of the corridor and passed through golden double doors into a wide, columned chamber. Motes of dust danced in the sunlight that spilled through the chamber and refracted from crystal chandeliers hanging high above. Gold and marble statuary lined the walls, and a great feasting table stretched down the chamber's middle.

'Where in the nether-realms is the stuntling?' cursed Hathrek in frustration. He had thought the Doomseeker somewhat cracked, but this was lunacy. He could not fathom how no one had yet discovered them, and at any moment he expected a tide of holy warriors to burst from all sides and bury him in blades. Sornsson would suffer for putting him through this, Hathrek vowed silently.

'Not just him,' responded Avanius with a frown in his voice. 'Where is anyone at all? If this is Sigmaron, where are my brother Stormcasts? Where are the scribes, the functionaries, the astromancers and cartologi?'

'Should we perhaps divide, try to find him more swiftly?' asked Eithweil, but Hathrek shook his head vehemently.

'I'm not being left alone in this place. Bad enough with a Stormcast to vouch for me. Without one, well...'

'Then we go that way,' said Avanius, pointing with his blade towards the huge double doors that led out from the chamber. 'It seems the most obvious route.'

They pressed on, emerging onto a wide spiralling stairway that ran both up and down from their landing. Its balustrade was engraved marble, twined with glimmering silver vines and twinkling star flowers. Warm golden light poured down the stairwell, falling through a stained glass ceiling high above.

'Now which way?' snarled Hathrek, exasperated. From above they heard the scuff of footsteps, and then a cry.

'Hello? Hello? Anyone?'

'Sornsson,' said Avanius, and set off up the steps at a run. Despite his heavy sigmarite plate, the Stormcast moved like a man unburdened, and it was all that Hathrek could do to keep up.

They reached the top of the spiralling stairway, having seen not another living soul, then dashed on across a vine-hung courtyard in which a beautiful fountain leapt and chuckled. Above, sunlight fell diffuse through crystal panes.

'This light is wrong,' Avanius called as they ran. 'Why do we not see open sky? Stars?'

'We're stuck in cursed Sigmaron, having been magicked through a portal from the hells-damned Silver Tower, chasing a deranged stuntling into who knows what danger, and you're worried about not being able to see the sky?' Hathrek was incredulous.

The two of them burst through another doorway and into a corridor, where they skidded to a halt. Sornsson stood ahead of them, before a tall, gilt-edged mirror. The Questor and the Darkoath advanced cautiously down the corridor, feet whispering across its rich mauve carpet. Eithweil swam into focus, drifting in their wake.

'Sornsson,' said Avanius carefully. 'Friend. Do not run again.' The duardin gave no response, continuing to stare with rapt fascination at the mirror's surface.

'Ho, stuntling,' shouted Hathrek angrily. 'You led us into Sigmaron. Sigmaron! You've most likely gotten me killed. What have you to say before I lop your head from your shoulders?'

Still the duardin did not speak.

'It is as though he hears us not,' whispered Eithweil. *'Strange.'*

'All of this is strange,' replied Avanius as they drew close to Sornsson. 'This place should be teeming with people. And the sky should be visible through every window, every pane... Sigmaron lies amidst the Heavens themselves. It swims between the stars, and celebrates that view of the firmament in every way. This vague, directionless sunlight – it's all wrong. I don't believe that...'

Just at that moment they drew close enough to see what Sornsson was staring at, and Avanius' words died on his tongue. There, swimming in the mirror's dark depths, sat a resplendent golden figure. His majesty was a physical force that almost drove them to their knees. The intensity of his gaze drew them in then scattered their thoughts like birds flying from a gunshot. There could be no denying the figure who manifested himself before them.

'Sigmar,' breathed Avanius, falling to one knee before the mirror. Hathrek's blade dangled, forgotten, in one hand as he stared at the God-King in awe. Some part of Hathrek's mind knew that he should have felt absolute dread, but only wonder filled his thoughts. Even the Mistweaver manifested herself fully, her blank mask turned quizzically towards the mirror's surface.

'Champions!' Sigmar's voice was a boom of thunder that shook Hathrek to his core. 'Companions!'

The Darkoath knelt alongside Avanius, his eyes desperately averted, while Sornsson stood and shook before the mirror.

'You walk the halls of Sigmaron when it is the tower you should seek!' The God-King's voice was dour, his brows drawn down. 'Knight-Questor Avanius, is your duty done? Have you defeated the master of the tower?'

Avanius shook his head. 'No, my God-King. We stepped through a portal…'

'And it brought you here!' finished Sigmar's booming voice, while lightning leapt and crackled in the darkness behind him. 'And with such strange company. Oathbreaker! Thrall of Chaos! Saih! By what right do you walk the halls of my realm?' Hathrek had no answer but to stare in mute fear at the golden figure before him. It seemed to grow by the moment, filling the surface of the mirror while the force of his presence bore down upon the chieftain like the weight of the moons and stars.

'Lord, they walk at my side,' said Avanius, voice firm despite the effort of enduring his God-King's wrath. 'They share my perils. They seek the end of the quest, just as I do.' For a moment, the apparition of Sigmar remained silent. Suddenly, it gave a booming laugh.

'Well spoken, Knight-Questor. You do not stray from your path, but perhaps it has strayed from you! A gift then, to align your fates once more. But know there will be bloodshed, before all is called to account.'

Sigmar raised one mighty hand, and within his grip they all saw a fragment of the amulet they sought. The apparition seemed almost to reach through the surface of the mirror. Upon a crackling cushion of energy, the amulet left Sigmar's grip and floated free, landing in Avanius' outstretched palm. Hathrek watched the Knight-Questor marvel at the artefact he now held. Then Avanius' pose stiffened, and he stared deep into the mirror.

'Lord,' he began, his voice heavy as he fought against the glamour that washed over him. 'What is wrong with this place? Where is everybody? Is this truly Sigmaron?'

At this, Sigmar was silent for a long moment. Then his eyes creased, and he boomed out a hearty laugh. The God-King's mouth opened wide, and mirth poured from him like water from a breaking dam. For a moment Hathrek felt moved to laugh as well, borne up by the force of deific amusement. But still the God-King laughed, and still his mouth yawned wider. Mirth became ferocity, and savage convulsions. The apparition warped out of focus for a moment, and when it resolved again its eyes had turned a terrible, jaundiced yellow. They multiplied across its forehead, popping open like blisters with black slit pupils. The Sigmar-thing's skin was webbed with squirming blue veins, and its lordly beard was transforming into something else. Something that resembled tentacles, or feathers. Needle fangs gleamed in its cruel grin, and the unmistakable aspect of the Gaunt Summoner appeared.

Hathrek recoiled from the mirror's churning surface as their nemesis revealed himself. Avanius cried out in horror, then the Darkoath swung his sword in a mighty arc and struck the mirror as hard as he could. The sense of being an animal caught in a trap had surged back in force, and Hathrek channelled all his fear and rage into the titanic blow. The mirror's surface shattered, the Gaunt Summoner giving a gleeful shriek before his image was obliterated.

Racing out from the point of impact, cracks spider-webbed the cursed mirror then, impossibly, spilled beyond it into the air itself. With a terrible crackling, crunching sound the walls and floor began to splinter apart. Reality was collapsing.

'*We have what we came for,*' urged Eithweil, breaking the spell of horror and bewilderment that had gripped them. '*We must depart the way we came. Swiftly.*' Avanius managed a stunned nod, but Sornsson reeled, his face distraught. Hathrek saw the duardin twitch and shudder, as though waking from some distant dream. Sornsson's jaw worked, and then he spun towards

Hathrek with a howl like a wounded animal. In the Doomseeker's eyes there swam a depth of absolute despair that was painful to see.

'You broke it,' screamed the duardin. 'You filthy Chaos worshipping *herkhnud*, you smashed it to pieces. I was out!' Hathrek backed away from the raging Fyreslayer, and the cracks that were now spreading perilously close. His own anger guttered before the raging inferno of Sornsson's maddened wrath.

'Stuntling. Sornsson. It wasn't real. None of it. It was a trap.'

But the Fyreslayer was insensible with rage and despair. Madness had taken him. Bellowing, Sornsson lunged towards Hathrek with his weapons raised. Moving with lightning speed, Avanius slammed his shield into the side of the duardin's head, clearly striking as hard as he dared. Sornsson toppled sideways, weapons spilling from nerveless hands. Quick as thought, Avanius scooped the Fyreslayer up and threw him over one shoulder before setting off down the corridor at a run. Following Avanius' lead, Hathrek snatched up Sornsson's axe and pick, before turning and dashing back the way they had come, away from the spreading cracks of oblivion.

Segments of wall fell away. Shards of sunlight splintered off and smashed upon the floor. Everywhere the illusion collapsed, it left a blank, black void behind it, haunted by the crooning laughter of the Gaunt Summoner.

Avanius dashed back across the courtyard, noting with disgust that the fountain had twisted into a fanged maw, which vomited gouts of jellied blue slime. The Fyreslayer was several hundred pounds of deadweight on his shoulder, and behind him reality was coming apart at the seams, but Avanius was Stormcast. He had been reforged with the might of the God-King in his veins. The true God-King. There was no test he could not endure, no challenge he could not defeat. And so he ran, armoured feet pounding marble as he started down the spiralling steps. Hathrek ran ahead. Of the Mistweaver there was no sign. From above came the terrible rending crashes of the stained glass ceiling tearing itself apart, while the steps shook and crumbled away by the moment. Ahead, a tumbling shard of reality the size of a dracoth punched through the stairway, Hathrek narrowly dodging its razor sharp edge. The shard ripped through marble, tearing a chasm fifteen feet across. Avanius kept going, and leapt without a second's thought. For a heart-stopping moment there was only nothingness beneath him. Then his feet slammed down on the steps and he kept running, Sornsson's weight bearing him down.

The companions dived through the huge doors into the banquet hall, only to be faced by a horrific sight. A feast had appeared along the tabletop, hideous delicacies of roasted corpses and squirming, tentacular things that spilled from crystal platters and squealed as they flailed blindly about. Daemons rose from their feast as the champions skidded to a halt. Maws stretched wide with gibbering glee. Mutating flames leapt from rubbery talons. In a mass, the Pink Horrors cartwheeled and capered forwards. Realising that the collapsing reality was right behind them, Avanius did the only thing he could. He charged.

The next few moments were a savage blur. Blades hacked and swung. Pink and blue fire leapt in liquid arcs, turning marble to oozing madness and gold to screaming mouths. Avanius barged aside a yammering thing with too many eyes, weaving desperately around a bolt of searing magic that roared within inches of his helm.

'There's too many,' yelled Hathrek, lopping the arm from a daemon, then stumbling as its other clubbing fist struck the side of his head. Blue fire washed across Avanius' breastplate, and he gasped in agony as he felt his flesh twist and split beneath the armour. Suddenly Eithweil was there, blasting into being above them amid a corona of black flame. Her voice spilled from the air in a roaring tide, booming out an incantation that sent the daemons reeling. As the shattering cracks spilled through the chamber's doorway, the Horrors spun and stumbled in confusion. Seizing their chance, Hathrek and Avanius fled, dashing between their discombobulated foes and making for the corridor in which the portal waited. Eithweil kept up her magic a few moments longer and as the racing cracks began to rend the foul daemons apart, Avanius saw her vanish in a whirl of smoke.

At last, the champions made it back to the portal corridor in time to see a dark figure diving through it ahead of them.

'Who…?' began Avanius.

'No time,' shouted Hathrek. 'Just move!' Seconds later, the golden tendrils of the portal lashed out once more, ripping them from their feet and bearing them willingly into the golden depths, away from the shattering pandemonium of the Heavens' death.

CHAPTER SIX

THE WEIGHT OF TRUTH

'Looks safe enough,' said Hathrek, feeling a profound sense of relief as he waved his blazing torch around the confined space. The flames growled and sputtered, throwing jagged shadows around the small chamber. Arachnid things with too many legs retreated from the light, folding themselves into cracks in the crystalline walls. Otherwise nothing moved, and there seemed only one way in or out of the crystalline oubliette.

'It is far from the false Heavens. It will serve,' replied Avanius, following the Darkoath Chieftain into the small room. Sornsson trudged in after him, one side of his face bruised and swollen. Eithweil was absent one moment, there the next, haunting the archway through which they had entered.

'I have woven what enchantments I am able here,' came her whisper. *'I cannot promise that they will fool everything that stalks these endless passages. The tower may undo what I have done.'*

'Thank you, Eithweil,' replied Avanius simply. 'Any measure of security is better than none.' The Stormcast limped to the far end of the crystal chamber and lowered himself into a sitting position with his back against the wall. Slowly, he reached up and unbuckled the straps of his battle helm, before lifting it free and placing it at his side. The face revealed was somehow younger than Hathrek had expected, its features strong and noble, but strange in a way he struggled to define. There was pain there, revealed in the tightness of the square jaw and lightning-blue eyes, but also an otherness that was profoundly unsettling. Hathrek was glad his companion normally went masked.

'You're injured,' Hathrek observed, endeavouring to keep his tone scornful. Avanius nodded, his breath rasping with fluid. His breastplate was scorched and warped out of shape where the daemonfires had struck him.

'We all are injured,' he replied.

'You're worse,' pressed Hathrek, seating himself against a different wall. 'So how does this work? Do you heal the way the rest of us do?'

'Do I heal?' echoed Avanius with a pained grunt of laughter. 'Like magic, you mean? Yes, I heal, far swifter than any mortal man. The gifts of our reforging help we Stormcasts to do so. The faith and purity of the Hallowed Knights seems to speed the process further. Given time, and a chance to rest.'

Sornsson had retreated to the room's darkest corner, and sat down heavily without a word. Now the battered duardin rummaged in his satchel and produced a crystal phial of softly glowing green liquid.

'This should help,' he muttered. 'Saw one before. With another group. Think you just drink it. Though knowing my luck, this one'll choke you.' The Fyreslayer tossed the small bottle to Avanius, who caught it and plucked out the stopper. The Stormcast held the phial to his lips and tipped his head back, swallowing the potion in a single swig. He gave several convulsive shudders, and lightning flickered about his body, then Avanius relaxed back against the wall with a sigh. Already Hathrek thought his breathing sounded easier.

'My thanks, Sornsson. You may have saved my life.'

The Fyreslayer nodded morosely, but said nothing.

For a time, the companions sat in silence, lost in their own thoughts. From far away came the echoing toll of a gong, then later some kind of shriek or hunting cry that faded slowly upon the still air. Eithweil remained in the doorway, folded half into its shadows so that she was barely visible. Hathrek even closed his eyes for a short while, but sleep remained elusive as it had since he came to the tower. Giving up, he drew his blade and laid it across his knees, before producing a whetstone and applying it to the sword's edge.

'So,' he said into the quiet, 'our brief hope of an escape didn't hold true. What do we do now?'

'We have eight segments of the amulet,' replied Avanius. 'We acquire the ninth, and then we conjure the Gaunt Summoner.'

'And we 'defeat' him?' asked Hathrek pointedly. The Knight-Questor nodded, his companion's meaning clearly not lost on him. 'We defeat him.'

'That will prove interesting,' mused the chieftain, continuing to run the whetstone along the edge of his blade.

'There's something else you need to do before that,' said Sornsson from his shadowed corner.

'Oh?' responded Hathrek in genuine surprise. 'And what would that be, stuntling? It doesn't involve knocking you senseless again does it?'

'Worse,' said Sornsson, not rising to the chieftain's bait. 'It involves killing me.' For a moment, the companions were silent, staring at Sornsson as though unsure of what they'd heard.

'I mean it,' pressed the duardin. 'I'm deadly serious. I'm oath-broke. I'm half mad. I'm no good to you. In fact, I'm a danger.'

'Sornsson,' began Avanius, 'you cannot mean that. You suffered a moment of weakness, that is all. It has passed.'

The duardin's eyes glinted coldly in the gloom. 'Passed, has it, Stormcast? He was nothing but bones and dust. You don't know how long it's been. Grimnir's beard, *I* don't know how long it's been. I just know I cannot remember my life before the tower. Nothing. Not the tunnels and halls of my lodge. Not my home. Companions, family, hopes… I try, now, but I cannot see my own father's face. All I can remember is this endless, shifting, lying bloody maze.'

Hathrek watched with disdain as a single tear tracked down the Fyreslayer's face, cutting through the grime and blood ground into his skin.

'I broke my oath. I failed my people. As punishment for that I have wandered this hell for so long that it has erased everything I ever cared about. But I'm done with my punishment. I've served my sentence. I don't want to live any more, and I don't want to spread my curse to any more poor fools unlucky enough to fall in with me.'

Sornsson subsided, his piece said. For a long moment, no one spoke, then Hathrek heaved a great sigh. He pushed himself to his feet, and hefted his sword.

'Fine,' said the chieftain airily. 'But I just whetted this blade. I hope you know your last deed in this life will be to dull the damn thing again with your spine.'

'You think this is some kind of joke?' snarled Sornsson, rising angrily from his corner.

'I do not,' replied Hathrek. 'I think this is a coward, taking the easy way out and spoiling the edge of my blade while he does so.'

Sornsson's expression was outrage.

'Coward?' he bellowed. 'Coward? I've been here longer than you've lived. I've fought and slain more foes than you can imagine. Trial after trial, time after time, no matter what I've forgotten or lost, I've carried on.'

'But not anymore,' replied Hathrek, swinging his blade in a deliberate arc as though practising a beheading. 'Giving up now, aren't you? I mean, you broke your oath all that time ago, and you lied to us about the amulet.'

'What madness are you spouting?' demanded Sornsson, his runes glowing with anger. 'I never knew about the damned amulet. Or if I did, I forgot. That was your mist witch over there, not me.'

Hathrek raised his eyebrows and nodded.

'It's true, you're right. You never knew about the amulet. Didn't know the way out. I understand. You're closer than you've been in years to escaping this place, but then, even if you did get out, you'd have to go back to your people with a broken oath. Better to let me lop your head off now.'

Sornsson paced his corner, shooting angry glares from under his beetled brows at the others.

'Don't think I don't see what you're doing, Chaos worshipper. Get me all wound up, convince me to keep fighting, that I'm going to get out. But you're right. I'm oathbroke, as I said. Nothing matters more to a Fyreslayer than his oath. It's everything we are.'

'What exactly was your oath, Sornsson?' asked Avanius. 'How did it break?'

'I swore an oath of safe passage for him that I watched over,' sighed the duardin, his anger seeming to drain away. He pulled a battered old ring from his pocket, turning it over between his thick fingers. 'I swore to act as a bodyguard, and to give my all for the safety of my ward. But the Scuttlings came from everywhere. They buried me in their wretched little bodies. I told him to stay close but he panicked. He ran. By the time I'd fought m'way free, he was feathered with arrows, and the scuttlers were gone.'

'Sounds like he was a fool and a coward,' said Hathrek sourly, meaning every word. 'Not worthy of your death.'

'Aye. Maybe,' replied Sornsson. 'But an oath's an oath. And by failing to protect him, and living on, I broke it. I'm good for naught but death now.'

'So be it,' exclaimed Hathrek. 'Kneel then and let me make it quick before I have to listen to any more of your whining.'

'Whining?' spat Sornsson, 'My oath…'

'Yes, it was binding and of utmost importance, we know,' interrupted Hathrek impatiently. 'My people make oaths too, duardin. Not to gold, or ancestors, or… beards, or whatever it is you stuntlings worship. We make our oaths to the Dark Gods.'

'Hathrek,' said Avanius warningly, but the chieftain pressed on.

'It's true, and you all know it. You know what my tattoos mean. We swear our oaths and we take them every bit as seriously as you duardin. More so, for if we fail, the consequences are horrible. The dead are the lucky ones. It's those that have to live with their punishment who truly suffer. The shamans say that no matter what shapes the gods might twist a man into, some part of him still remembers what he was.' Hathrek's eyes were distant for a moment, haunted by something unspoken. 'But there's no going back. No making good on your mistakes. We who swear the dark oaths get no second chances.'

'Are you implying that I do?' asked Sornsson.

'Well don't you?' cried Hathrek angrily. 'You still live, despite all the odds. You still have your strength, and your blades.' Sornsson looked down at his weapons, discarded in the gloom. 'You swore an oath to give your all safeguarding someone through the tower,' Hathrek continued. 'Never mind that you couldn't have known the risks you were taking, or what an impossible, hellish place you consigned yourself to. You took that oath, and you've suffered the punishment for your failure. But you still live, and unlike all those whose paths to glory ended in madness and death, you still have a chance to atone.' Hathrek was animated, jabbing with the point of his blade to emphasise each point. 'We are here, now, mortal beings that the tower seeks to slay. Even Eithweil... I think. We seek to be done with this maze, and escape with our lives. And the gods know, we're likely to see our own blood shed before this thing is done. So make a new oath to us. I swear to you on all that is sacred to me that I will gladly let you step in front of the first blade that swings my way, if it would bring you peace.'

Sornsson was nodding slowly, and cinders danced upon his breath.

'A new oath,' he muttered. 'I could do that. And make it a death-oath. If I fail this time, I take my own life as penance.'

'So then, everybody dies, what could be better,' exclaimed Hathrek sardonically, but he could see that Sornsson was warming to the idea now. He had not become his tribe's chieftain by winning battles with blades alone.

'Mock all you like, Hathrek of the Gadalhor, but you're right. I've spent so long dwelling on my failings and trying to flee my mistakes that I never saw the chance I had to make it right.' The duardin hefted his pick. Slowly, deliberately, he levered one of the runes from the flesh of his forearm. Blood squirted and skin tore, but he persisted, teeth gritted against the pain. Finally, the ur-gold came loose, and he held it up before them, panting.

'On this,' the duardin instructed urgently. 'Take my oath on this before its magic fades.' Hathrek took the bloodied rune with a grimace.

'What do I...?'

'Just hold it out, like that, that's right.' Sornsson laid his heavy palm over the rune that glowed faintly in Hathrek's hand. The chieftain recognised the solemnity of this moment and set aside his usual mockery as the duardin pressed ahead.

'I swear, by my ancestors, by my father, by the Volturung and by Grimnir, that I shall see you, my companions, safely through the Silver Tower even if it costs me my life. And I swear that, should I fail, my life will be forfeit. Do you so witness?'

Hathrek nodded.

'Yes,' said Avanius, his tone neutral.

'*This I witness,*' came Eithweil's voice, floating on the air.

'Then it's done,' grinned Sornsson, looking younger and more vital than he had since they had met him. 'It's no proper oath-binding, but you are witnesses as honour demands, and the runes felt its truth. I'll see you through, or I'll die in the attempt.'

Avanius half listened as Hathrek brushed off the duardin's excitement with some sardonic comment. The chieftain sat himself back down, muttering that he was determined to get some sleep if no one else was planning to kill themselves just now. Sornsson began to sharpen his blades, steel in his eyes where there had been only sorrow. Avanius knew the Fyreslayer was not fool enough to miss the manipulation, that he had been talked into swearing a new oath and seeking atonement. But then, the Stormcast felt sure that the duardin had wanted precisely that. His despair had hidden the desperate need for another chance, one that he had been afraid of seizing lest it too end in defeat. It had shaken Avanius' certainties to the core when Hathrek, of all people, had spotted that need. The Knight-Questor had learned respect for Hathrek's abilities as a warrior since they had begun their adventure together. Until now he had not truly seen the Darkoath's potential as a leader.

It was a tragedy that one with such strength in him had been lost to the worship of the Dark Gods. It was sorrowful that the chieftain seemed set upon a path that would see him take the dark gifts of the Gaunt Summoner. Even if Hathrek truly believed that he did so for his people, he would only be leading them, and himself, into damnation. If Sigmar had only been able to reach Hathrek first…

For a long moment Avanius sat very still as his head spun with revelation. 'Only the faithful,' he murmured, the steadying mantra of his Stormhost. 'Only the faithful. Only the faithful.' How could he have been such a fool? Was he not pious enough? Wise enough? Had his latest reforging robbed him of his wits? How had he not seen the task that was before him this whole time?

Avanius' orders had been precisely worded, brief in the extreme but without ambiguity. Or so he had thought. *Defeat the master of the Silver Tower*. And of course, the Knight-Questor had believed that he must find the Gaunt Summoner and slay him. But now Avanius found revelation. According to what small lore the Stormcast Eternals possessed regarding the Gaunt Summoners, it was believed that, upon the ninth day after the death of such a daemon, a new one would rise from the Crystal Labyrinth of Tzeentch to take its place. Avanius knew that, and until now he had believed that Sigmar had a wider plan that depended upon this creature's death. Perhaps its demise would upset the webs of fate that such servants of Tzeentch wove. Perhaps it would act as a message, a statement that even within the most impenetrable strongholds those who served Chaos were not safe. But now, Avanius realised with a shock that securing the Summoner's death would be nothing but a pyrrhic victory, because his true quest was both more difficult and more subtle than that. The God-King did not want the daemon slain. He wanted it *defeated*. And as he thought upon the strength and glimmers of nobility that he had seen within Hathrek, Avanius finally knew how he must secure that defeat.

The Hallowed Knight let his new clarity flow through him and lend strength to the magic within his body as they laboured to heal him. Just a few hours of rest, he thought, and he would have the strength to finish the task that he had been set.

'I will do my duty, my liege,' he murmured. 'I will not let the daemon win.'

Like a wraith, Eithweil lingered in the archway of the chamber and let her mind wander free along the winding ways of the tower. Its complexity was maddening, but she could sense the song of the final fragment, like a silver thread leading her on through the darkness. And she could hear, too, the ever-present whispers of the tower. Its corrupting influence. Its silent lies. Her champions were not aware of the insidious voices. They had not the breadth of perception to sense them, nor to resist. What changes would the tower have wrought already upon these poor creatures? How far had their minds been twisted? With what had they been tempted, in the darkest hollows of their minds? It was impossible for even a Mistweaver Saih to know such things, but she sensed that they must hurry. Perhaps the Stormcast had some measure of protection. Perhaps. But they were all of them saturated with the tower's corruption, and the longer they lingered, the worse that would become.

Moreover, she thought, there was the vermin creature that followed them. How long before it decided to strike again, as it had in the temple when it slew the priest? Just another secret she had kept from her champions. But then, truth was like gold. It seemed so precious, so important to possess. But how quickly it grew heavy, while its value was all a matter of perception. No, she mused. They needed know no more than they already did to serve her ends. After that, their lives were of no consequence to her. Not that they ever had been.

CHAPTER SEVEN

THE FINAL TRIAL

When the group broke camp once more, Skrytchwhisker was ready. He had lurked in a nearby chamber, ear to the wall to catch the vibrations of their movements. Thus when they set out, the Deathrunner was ready. Skrytchwhisker had to admit, as he slipped out of the strange little store-room, that he impressed even himself. How long had he been now without food or water, or sleep? A long time, he knew that much. Yet still he persisted. Such endurance. Such fortitude, without even the gnaw-pangs of hunger to distract him. Truly, thought the assassin, he was the greatest Eshin operative of his age. Perhaps of all ages.

Filled with pride and confidence, saturated with the promises of the Silver Tower, the skaven trailed after his quarry. Down, they went, through endless passages, and stairways, and shimmering portals. Through a network of interlinked clockwork crawl-spaces where jets of flame spat from gargoyles' maws, and death seemed always a moment away. Across a ragged chasm full of wheeling stars and glaring eyes, over which arched a breathtaking crystal ceiling crisscrossed by inverse rivers of quicksilver. Into the fresco-daubed chambers of a Chaos-thing cult, leaving the Tzeentch-worshippers' bodies strewn and bloody before their twisted altar. Diminutive magical beings dogged the group's steps at times. Once, while scrambling along a half-submerged passage of crumbling stonework, Skrytchwhisker found himself eye to surprised eye with something that resembled a fish, but with the legs of an imp. The creature boggled at him for a moment, then was gone, slithering away into a broken pipe. Skrytchwhisker shook his head, marvelling at the strangeness of this place, before pressing on through the dripping gloom after his prey.

Finally, after what seemed an age, the assassin watched his victims clamber through the yawning jaws of a huge stone wyrm, and slide away into the darkness of its gullet. Skrytchwhisker gave them a steady count to get clear, then flicked out his climbing spikes and scuttled after them.

At the bottom of the long, perilous descent, Hathrek slid from another stone maw and into a noisome cavern. He sprang quickly to his feet, blade out, only to feel something plaster itself across his face. Revolted, the chieftain clawed at the substance and ripped it away. In the half-light thrown by glowing crystal outcroppings, he saw his fist was full of sticky strands.

'Spider's web,' he muttered, as his companions came to their feet behind him.

'*Worse, I fear*,' replied Eithweil as she flickered into being at his side. '*Scuttlings.*' The Mistweaver gestured to the ceiling. Up there, Hathrek saw clotted masses of webbing squirming with frantic movement. Already he could see the strange greenskins slithering from amidst their webs, beady red eyes staring from ragged black cowls. Hathrek cursed as one of the creatures nocked an arrow to its bow and let fly. The Darkoath smacked the arrow from the air with the flat of his blade, seeing more Scuttlings bursting from their web-nest by the second. They were descending on fibrous strands and squeezing from cracks in the walls, scurrying on their many legs.

'There's a lot of them,' said Hathrek in warning.

'Not enough,' responded Sornsson, a killing light gleaming in his eyes.

'The amulet,' called Avanius, pointing with his blade to the web-nest above. 'The last piece is up there, see?' Sure enough, a jewel glinted amid the smothering strands.

'Then let's take it,' grinned Hathrek with a surge of excitement, sidestepping another crude arrow before launching into a charge.

Sornsson hurled himself into the fight with murderous relish. Here were the creatures that had forced him into breaking his oath, so long ago. His hate for them burned as hot now as it had on that awful day, and no amount of their blood would quench it. Still, with every pick and axe blow that crunched into green flesh, the Doomseeker felt bone-deep satisfaction.

More Scuttlings poured into the chamber by the moment, a yammering, shrieking tide of attackers. Many shot stubby arrows at the champions, though the spider-legged grots' aim was poor enough that they hit their own more often than their foes. Avanius' shield rang with the impact of rock-tipped projectiles. Sornsson felt more than one arrow sheathe itself in his flesh, but he broke the shafts off almost without thought and ploughed on through the melee. The Scuttlings came on in a mass, burying the invaders in scrabbling limbs and rusty blades, but the champions fought furiously. They were close to their prize now, and nothing would stop them. Sornsson fought like a warrior possessed. His eyes blazed with fire and his runes glowed white hot until flames trailed after pick and axe. Every swing of the Doomseeker's weapons saw another swathe of Scuttlings smashed through the air. Sornsson's cries of wrath were incoherent, but for the first time in an age, his thoughts ran clear.

'No broken oaths this time, eh stuntling?' laughed Hathrek, bleeding from half a dozen shallow wounds as he spitted two more Scuttlings with a lunge of his blade. Sornsson roared in reply, almost feeling a kind of warrior comradeship with the Darkoath, then windmilled his way through the press of his foes.

Through the maelstrom of battle drifted the Mistweaver. She rose through the carnage as though at the eye of a hurricane, mask tilted towards the amulet fragment in its prison of webs. Its song filled her mind, rising in chorus with the eight segments already in her possession. It was a siren song, filling her up and compelling her to make the fragments whole once more. Even with all of her sorcerous might, and her exceptional mental focus, the Mistweaver could not have resisted that call even if she had tried.

Scuttlings came at her from every side, but her powers flickered in a dark corona that drove them mad. Greenskins fell upon one another with curved blades, or tore out their own throats while choking with deranged laughter. More simply fled, consumed by unreasoning terror. Their dismay spread like a sickness through those still fighting below, until quite suddenly the swirling melee became a frantic rout. Scuttlings who, a moment before, had been hacking and stabbing madly at the invaders in their nest, now turned and fled as their nerve failed them. Bleeding from dozens of cuts and bites, the champions gave chase. They hacked down more of the scrambling creatures by the moment. As swiftly as it had begun, the fight was over. The rocky floor was carpeted with hacked and mangled corpses, while the last few wounded Scuttlings tried to drag themselves to the cracks and bolt-holes through which their tribe had fled. Sornsson moved between these luckless creatures, dripping with greenskin blood as he stamped viciously upon their heads and crushed their skulls one by one.

'Remind me never to make you break an oath,' commented Hathrek dryly, watching the Fyreslayer execute his helpless victims. Eithweil ignored them as she ripped aside the web-strands with her staff, and snatched the amulet fragment from the air as it fell.

Behind the group, in the shadows of the dragon's maw, beady red eyes watched in anticipation as the aelf-witch drifted slowly back to the ground with her treasure. The Deathrunner had slain a number of green scuttle-things himself during the fight, flicking poisoned blades at them from hiding and gambling that the group would be too preoccupied to notice his aid. Skrytchwhisker need not have worried, as all eyes were on the floating mage.

'Eithweil,' said the lightning-man, 'we should gather our wits and ready ourselves before...'

'*No*,' came the mage-thing's voice, a distant, distracted whisper on the air that sent shivers of fear along Skrytchwhisker's spine. '*We cannot wait. It sings so beautifully, Stormcast. Do you not hear? The song must be completed. It yearns.*'

The tattooed barbarian stepped forwards, raising a hand.

'Wait a moment witch, Avanius is right.'

'*No*,' came the aelf-witch's voice again, angry now. '*No. We swim in the river of fate, and to fight the current is to drown. The song must soar...*'

With that, the mage-thing brought the incomplete amulet from amidst her robes and raised it high. The others lunged for her and, though he did not truly understand what was happening, Skrytchwhisker found himself sharing their panic. Without even looking around, the mage-thing swept one hand out and the warriors fell back, screaming as though in terrible pain. The assassin saw the duardin look up from his methodical murder as the aelf-witch raised the last segment of the amulet and, with a sigh that echoed around the chamber, slid it into place. Magical energies flashed, lines of liquid gold seared along the edges of the final segment, making the amulet whole once more. A pulse of blue fire leapt outwards, and for a moment Skrytchwhisker's prey were driven back, blinded and deafened by sorcerous energies. In the dragon's maw, Skrytchwhisker shrank back, wreathed in the musk of fear.

Avanius blinked his sight clear of blinding smears as the magical flames died out. The companions stared in dread at the black, sucking hole where the amulet had been moments before. Eithweil backed away from the fist-sized rent in reality, shaking her helmed head as though waking from a dream.

A hand came first, long fingers slithering from the hole. An arm followed, then another and another. Blue, shimmering cloth spilled out in an impossible tide, and an awful crooning filled the air. Looking desperately at one another, the champions readied their weapons and backed slowly away. Like some awful spider, unfolding itself from a gap through which it simply should not have fit, the Gaunt Summoner slithered into reality. The purity of his disgust for this creature of Chaos filled Avanius with righteous purpose.

The daemon's many eyes fixed upon them. His black tongue slithered over his needle fangs, and he gave a sigh that crawled across their skin like flensing knives.

'You are heeeere…' he whispered.

'We are here to defeat you,' said Avanius, head high and blade crackling despite the thing's unspeakable aura. The daemon turned towards him, and the Knight-Questor gritted his teeth as a squirming feeling of disgust knotted his insides.

'Mmmyessss….' hissed the daemon. 'The noble knight. So sure of his purity, so certain of his task. So ssssorely deceived.' The Summoner's gaze swept on, transfixing each companion in turn like an insect upon a pin.

'The oath-bound one. Desperate to die. Anxious to live. The seeker after power, telling himself he fights for his people even as he drownssss in his father's shadow.' Hathrek flinched at this, lips pulling back in an unconscious snarl.

'And the witch. The shadowmassssster. The deceiver,' leered the Summoner, his many eyes resting on Eithweil. 'Ssso clever, to cage a daemon. Ssso clever to steal its secrets. Secrets it sought alwaysssss to reveal.' The Summoner dangled long, taloned fingers like a man working the strings of a puppet. 'Every sssstep of the way…' Avanius saw Eithweil shake her head slowly, a gesture of dazed denial.

'Lies!' boomed Avanius, though he could be certain of no such thing. 'You lie to make us doubt ourselves. You lie to make us fear. You lie because you are a daemon of Tzeentch and it is all you know. But we shall not listen to your filth, creature. We shall only strike you down.'

The daemon's leer widened until it seemed his head must split in two.

'You may try,' he sneered. 'But in my realm, you are powerlessss. Come, follow me if you can. I will show you the paths of fate.'

With that, the Summoner spun and swept his staff out in an arc. Kaleidoscopic light spilled into the cavern as the skin of reality split beneath the blow, yawning wide. The champions cried out and lunged towards the daemon. As they did, another figure, dark and sinuous, gave a shriek and burst from hiding in the dragon's maw. None was quick enough as, with a hideous chuckle of glee, the daemon vanished through the rent he had torn.

'Don't let him escape,' yelled Sornsson as he ran forwards. 'He's the only way out of this place!'

At the same moment, Hathrek turned with a curse towards the verminous, dagger-wielding figure that had suddenly sprung into their midst. He swung his sword but the skaven rolled under the blow, diving through the glowing rent.

'What…?' began Hathrek in bewilderment.

'No time to tarry, just move,' barked Avanius, spurring the chieftain to dash forwards.

As her champions vanished into the glowing rent, only Eithweil was left, still hanging in the chamber before the shimmering rift. The Mistweaver shook her head again, surrounded by a susurrus of whispers. Anger. Denial. Confusion. Panic. They all echoed down to a single point. Rage. Burning like a star of black light, the Mistweaver Saih summoned all her energies and surged in pursuit.

Reality bucked and twisted around the champions as they chased after the Summoner. Sornsson found himself running along a crystal corridor, feet barely touching the ground as it tilted madly downwards. Ahead, a skaven in the black garb of an assassin was scrambling along one wall, scuttling with maddened speed after the vanishing figure of the Gaunt Summoner. Sornsson ran furiously, frantic not to lose his quarry. The corridor seemed to stretch out forever, tumbling over itself as it did, and the Doomseeker cried out as the walls shattered away like glass. Beyond he saw the corridor repeated again and again, as though reflected through the facets of a crystal. There he saw himself, running wildly after his daemonic tormentor. Sometimes he was alone. Sometimes he was wounded.

Sometimes he was not there at all. For a moment his mind reeled as the impossible vista exploded before him, myriad shards of fate crowding in and threatening to drive him mad. Instead the duardin cursed and ran on, eyes fixed on his foe.

Hathrek ran hard, arms and legs pumping madly, heart hammering in his chest. He saw the duardin vanish through a shattering swirl of crystal fragments, and dived after him. It didn't matter what he had to do now, thought the chieftain. What he had to face. What madness the daemon threw at him. Power and glory were so close. Everything his father had lost when he devolved into that thing and left his horrified eldest son to take the reins of power. Everything his tribe had expected of him, everything they had demanded. Everything they didn't deserve. Hathrek would take it all, walk his own path to glory. And unlike the fool that came before him, he would not fail.

Suddenly, Hathrek was falling, tumbling headlong into a churning lake of quicksilver. He splashed down into the liquid metal, screwing his eyes tight shut and holding his breath in the moment before it engulfed him. Cloying, ice-cold weight pressed in all around. Total disorientation gripped him. Hathrek struggled, thrashing against the thick, freezing slop as the breath burned in his lungs and panic fought to drown his thoughts. A hand was suddenly grasping his, pulling, dragging him upwards through the metallic mire until he burst from its surface with a whooping gasp. Hathrek tasted metal as he thumped onto his side, scrabbling the quicksilver from his eyes. Avanius stood over him, dripping with liquid metal and shimmering with lightning. His cloak was gone, as was his shield. Behind him, Hathrek saw that the chamber had no ceiling, just an endless spiral of stars and stairways. His gorge rose at the sight.

'Come,' growled Avanius from behind his expressionless mask, as he hauled Hathrek to his feet. 'We're not done yet.'

Hathrek stood, swiping more silver from his eyes, and nodded before following Avanius at a run through the chamber's only arch.

As the Summoner twisted the rules of his impossible realm at will, the champions ran down mirrored stairways that folded in upon themselves over and over again. They leapt yawning chasms of spinning clockwork and crackling magical energies. They chased the Summoner through chambers they had seen, and chambers they had not. They saw themselves face terrible fates that had not come to pass, failing where they had prevailed. Still they ran, refusing to allow any amount of magical trickery to turn them from their course. They endured sights that would have driven lesser minds to madness, and they felt their sanity fraying as they dashed on through the endless gauntlet of madness and illusion. Yet still they ran.

The assassin scurried with them, sometimes ahead, sometimes behind. In one chamber, the skaven and the Fyreslayer burst through opposite doorways at the same moment and a vicious fight ensued amid spinning blocks of screaming crystal. The duardin swore as a green-venomed blade ripped across his chest, leaving an ugly black wound in its wake. The assassin hissed in pain as the Doomseeker's axe lopped the tip off his tail, and clipped one of his ears from his head. As the two foes hacked at one another, the whole room twisted around them into a sluicing whirlpool that sent them tumbling down into a dark abyss.

On and on it went, until at last the champions and their verminous shadow plunged through a spinning maelstrom of flame and tumbled out into a cavern that sang with power. Huge crystals of amber and amethyst jutted from the uneven floor, creating a glittering forest that stretched away into a distant haze. Purple and blue storm clouds boiled high above, the crystal-studded ceiling of the cavern visible in glimpses through their churning mass.

Sornsson rose, feeling the burning pain of the wound in his chest. A glance confirmed that black fingers of corruption were spreading slowly out from it, and green pus was welling around its edges. With a curse, the Fyreslayer cast around for the authors of his woes, but neither the Summoner nor the skaven could be seen. There were only the champions, and the thrumming crystals within whose depths phantoms swirled.

'Is this real?' asked Avanius, rising painfully to his feet.

'Is any of it?' replied Sornsson.

'All and none,' came the whisper of the Saih. *'Tricks and lies that write a truth we none of us would wish.'* Her voice sang with anger, and something else. Bitterness, thought Sornsson – maybe even shame.

'If the Summoner tricked you,' rumbled the Fyreslayer, surprising himself with the calmness of his voice, 'then he tricked us all. This is the tower. It's all just lies. Perhaps he was never here at all?'

'He was here,' spat Hathrek, brandishing his blade. 'He's still here. Aren't you?' he roared to the storm clouds above. 'This is just another accursed test, isn't it? See if we'll give up? Go mad? Never! If I have to walk a thousand thousand leagues through this place, I will find you and you will kneel before me! I will never, ever give up!'

A hissing laugh filled the air in reply, a slithering, spine-chilling gale of mirth. Above, the clouds twisted into the leering visage of the Gaunt Summoner, and flickers of lightning flashed in place of fangs.

'Gooood,' came his voice, a tide of oil and bile to drown their senses. 'Yessss. One last test. And then, you may claim what you came for. Master thissss, and master fate itself...'

The clouds rent and tore apart. Energy crackled madly from one crystal to the next, arcing together. There was a blinding flash, and then a hulking figure stood before them. Sornsson watched as it rose to its full height, furnace light glowing from eyes, mouth, and the crawling sigils that decorated its flesh. A familiar crown of curving horns spread from the huge beast's brow, while its muscles seemed to squirm and writhe beneath its blue-fleshed hide. Steam rose from the hulking humanoid figure, and as it raised its staff the thing threw back its head and gave vent to a ground-shaking roar.

'Did we not kill this thing way back down the road?' gasped Sornsson, bewildered. 'It looks like the beast from the fungus cave.'

'Same one, I think,' said Hathrek, backing away. 'Only this time it's possessed.'

'We killed it once,' growled Avanius. 'We shall kill it again. No more games.' Eithweil did not speak. Instead she levelled her staff and blasted a jet-black bolt of energy at the creature.

The beast-wizard spun, sorcerous light pouring from its eyes, and raised one huge hand in a warding gesture. The Mistweaver's magical blast exploded into inky smoke, the detonation rippling back along its length and slamming into Eithweil. The Saih was blown backwards through the air, striking a crystal with a sickening crunch. Sornsson winced at the sound.

Hathrek gave a wordless roar and launched himself at the monster. His blade swept down, only to be snatched in mid-air. It cut into the beast's palm, liquid light dribbling from the wound. Hathrek fought to wrench his blade free, only for the beast to kick him square in the chest. The breath whooshed from his lungs as the Darkoath was propelled backwards, skidding to a stop some way distant. He coughed in agony as he tried to stand, blood flecking his lips.

Avanius and Sornsson attacked as one, lunging in from opposite directions. The beast-wizard swept its staff around to block Avanius' blade in an explosion of light and lightning. Sornsson sank his axe deep into its bicep, releasing a spray of liquid fire and eliciting a bellow of pain. The beast backhanded the duardin, and Sornsson's world exploded in agony. As his senses returned he realised he was sprawled some distance from the fight, staring up at the turbulent clouds and feeling broken teeth shifting loose in his mouth.

The Doomseeker staggered to his feet in time to see the monster turn its full fury upon Avanius. The possessed beast summoned a crackling blast of magic at the tip of its staff and fired it into the Stormcast's chest. Sigmarite plate buckled with the force of the impact, and Avanius staggered back, wreathed in white-orange flame. Sornsson felt his respect for the Hallowed Knight redouble as, shrugging off the blow, Avanius drove forwards again, catching the meteoric downswing of the beast's staff on his pauldron and ramming his sword into its chest.

Glowing ichor splattered from the hideous wound, and the beast roared in pain before punching Avanius full in the face. The Questor's faceplate cracked with the force of the blow and he was smashed off his feet, falling spread-eagled before the monster. The beast grasped the hilt of Avanius' sword and wrenched it from its wound, before flinging it contemptuously away. It raised one huge hoof, ready to stamp down on Avanius' head. For an instant, Sornsson was afraid that he would once more be too far away, too slow, to aid his companions. Before the creature's hoof could come crashing down, another bolt of smoke and shadow bloomed. The monster roared in fury, beams of light spearing through the winding mass of darkness that engulfed it. It lashed out at half-seen phantasms with its savage sorcery. Eithweil staggered closer with her staff levelled.

Slowly, falteringly, the beast dropped to its knees. It roared in fury and confusion as the Mistweaver redoubled her attack, one hand holding her staff level, the other clutched to a bleeding rent in her robes. She was limping, one leg twisted, but still she poured her powers into her furious assault. Sornsson dared to hope that it would be enough.

Then the beast-wizard gave a mighty bellow and raised its own staff. Amber fire flared like a new sun, exploding the shroud of shadow and illusion. The beast lurched to its feet, liquid light dribbling from mouth, eyes and snout. It pounded forwards three swift, lunging steps, and punched its fist through Eithweil's chest almost to the elbow. Sornsson cried out in denial, charging towards the hideous tableau with his weapons raised. The Mistweaver shuddered as she was hoisted high, the beast bellowing flaming hate at her as she convulsed. Inky blood rained down, turning to smoke as it struck the ground. Silently, without even a final whisper, Eithweil turned to shadow and vapour and vanished from sight.

For a split second, the monster's bestial features twisted into a leer of victory, before Hathrek's blade whistled down and lopped off its right arm. The beast reeled, trying to turn as glowing gore jetted from the stump. The Darkoath's blade swung again, ripping the other arm away.

'Enough!' roared Hathrek, lashing his sword across the thing's guts and spilling ropes of glowing light. 'Enough!' he screamed again as he lopped the beast's head from its shoulders, releasing a geyser of flame. 'Enough!' the chieftain bellowed one last time, hacking his sword into his collapsing foe again and again until luminescent blood sprayed in all directions and nothing remained but twitching meat. Panting, the Darkoath

Chieftain stepped back from the mangled remains of his victim. As he did so, the last of its carcass burst into flames, dissolving into a glowing pool. Sornsson joined Hathrek at its edge, as did Avanius. Through the pool's surface, another place could be seen, a warped reflection of the temple in which Masudro had died so long ago.

'Enough…' agreed the mocking voice of the Gaunt Summoner from the clouds above. 'Come, champions, and claim your reward.'

Limping, battered, bloody, the three survivors looked at one another solemnly.

'She did not die in vain,' croaked Sornsson. The Fyreslayer was unsure what he felt at Eithweil's loss, for he had neither trusted nor liked the witch. Yet a comrade had fallen and he had not been able to die in her stead. For that, at least, he was sorry.

'Agreed,' nodded Avanius.

One by one, they stepped through the portal to meet their destiny. At their backs, a dark shape detached itself from the lee of a towering crystal and flowed in their wake one last time.

CHAPTER EIGHT

INTO THE FIRE

The companions found themselves surrounded by roaring flame. Heat beat down upon them in hammerblows. The glare dazzled them. Squinting, they took in their surroundings. Once more, the huge Tzeentchian temple spread out on all sides, though so much had changed that only intuition told them they stood in the same place as before. Where once the walls had been formed of precious metals and crystal shards, now they were squirming flesh, moaning faces that screamed their madness from between waving tentacles and gnashing maws. Instead of prisms, huge brass gargoyles were set into the floor. From the maw of each jetted streams of warp flame, searing columns that rose to the ceiling like dancing tornadoes, then flowed together to create a storm of fire. Within those leaping flames, daemonic entities screamed and capered, cackling in glee to see the wounded mortals enter their domain.

Across the vast temple, twisted by false perspective into a looming and godlike figure, the Gaunt Summoner waited. He had taken the place of the statue they had destroyed, a living effigy in place of a lifeless idol. Where the statue's taloned feet had once been planted, now there was a broad golden dais, at the centre of which stood a rune-carved arch. Energy flickered and danced in that mystic doorway, and the Gaunt Summoner stood before it like a guardian.

'The way out,' rumbled Sornsson.

'Looks like it,' replied Hathrek. 'But before that, the Summoner.' He looked at Avanius. 'Seems like we come to it at last, Stormcast.'

Avanius shook his head. 'Not quite yet, Hathrek. It appears our host has not finished testing us after all.' The companions followed Avanius' pointing blade. The Summoner had raised his staff high, and his mouth was moving in some dark chant. As he spoke, the pillars of flame that supported the blazing ceiling flexed and surged, and daemonic creatures began to spring from their midst. The pink-fleshed Horrors cartwheeled across the temple floor, trails of flame springing up behind them as they gathered in a gibbering mass before the Summoner's dais.

'Oh what now?' snarled Hathrek. 'You said we were done, creature,' he bellowed at the Gaunt Summoner. If the distant daemon gave any indication of hearing, it was only to grin cruelly in response.

'One last charge then,' grinned Sornsson mirthlessly. The Fyreslayer hefted his weapons and spat a cracked tooth onto the temple floor. 'You'll live to get out, I'll make damn sure of it.'

'We all will,' replied Avanius. 'The Gaunt Summoner will not best us.'

Hathrek and Sornsson nodded, and the three of them advanced towards the daemons that barred their path between the columns of flame.

'For Grimnir!' roared Sornsson.

'For Sigmar!' bellowed Avanius.

Hathrek just shot his comrades a wry grin, then led the charge.

Hathrek and his companions advanced across the temple floor as quickly as they could. They leapt over trenches of seething warp fire, and dodged bolts of sorcery hurled by the daemons gathered before them. Hathrek plucked the last few throwing axes from his belt, one at a time, and sent them whipping end-over-end into their unnatural foes. Nothing would stop him now, not so close to his prize. Wherever one of those spinning blades hit home, a daemon of Tzeentch split in two. Sulphurous flames leapt and sorcery sparked the air as blue simulacra squirmed, grumbling, from the melting bodies of their predecessors. For all Hathrek's efforts, the daemon throng was undiminished, and the Summoner's oily mirth filled the air as the creatures sprang forwards to meet the champions. Hathrek saw Sornsson scorched by a blast of unnatural fire, burned to the bone all down one side of his jaw. Though this looked agonising, and black threads of corruption laced the flesh of his chest, the dogged Fyreslayer kept going. Avanius was smashed from his feet by a bolt of magic, and for a horrible moment Hathrek thought him slain. Yet the Hallowed Knight hauled himself back to his feet with a pained snarl, lightning spilling from a fresh tear in his armour. He roared out another war cry to Sigmar and advanced once more, trailing droplets of spectral flame.

Only the Darkoath seemed untouched. The daemons' fire spilled around him, but sputtered and died as several of his skull-like tattoos blazed with blood-red light. He laughed wildly as he ran, face twisted in a mask of mad joy as jabbering dismay spread through his foes. He could hear the booming laughter of Dark Gods, and feel the skin-tingling closeness of true power.

'This is my moment,' he roared. 'The Dark Brothers see me, and their blessings are mine!' Yelling a war cry to his patrons, praying for their strength, the Darkoath Chieftain ploughed into the daemons with his blade swinging. A thing with avian eyes and a gaping maw came at him, trying to tangle his blade with its lashing tongues. Hathrek lopped the grisly appendages off in a spray of ichor, then rammed his sword right down the thing's throat. Its eyes bulged, before it burst apart in a gout of flame. Talons bit into his flesh and tentacles lashed him, yet still Hathrek fought on like a man possessed.

To his left, Hathrek saw Sornsson charge between two Blue Horrors and smash them both flat with his outswung weapons. The Fyreslayer spun in a tight circle, ripping his axe up through the inverted face of another freakish daemon, before sinking his pick into the eye-socket of a fourth. To the right, Avanius wielded his sword two-handed, lopping the gangling arms from a chanting Horror before it could conjure more flames to hurl.

Hathrek's muscles burned with exertion, his wounds with pain, but still he fought, impaling another daemon before ripping his blade out and through the face of yet another. The air was so hot that it scorched his lungs as he breathed. Still the Darkoath and his companions would not give up, and one by one the daemons of Tzeentch were chopped apart. At last there remained nothing but capering sprites of yellow flame that the champions stamped and smashed into oblivion. The last entities fled back to their columns of fire, spitting incomprehensible vitriol as they retreated.

Panting and bloodied, Hathrek looked defiantly up at the Gaunt Summoner. The daemon stared back, his mocking leer wiped away. Baring his fangs, the Summoner levelled his staff at them and began a new, darker incantation.

* * *

Sornsson could feel the energy draining from his limbs. His burned face was pure agony, and he could barely see from one eye. Worse was the steady, throbbing ache of the wound in his chest. He could taste its poison now, and where the black tendrils spread out beneath his skin, his runes were being extinguished one by one.

The Summoner was readying yet another spell, his staff glowing with power as tendrils of flame whipped down from on high to wind about him. Sornsson had a feeling that, if this was the daemon's last gambit, it would be a deadly one. Their nemesis was no longer playing games. He wanted them dead. Well, the daemon could have his life, and help him fulfil his oath at the same time. Sornsson knew, deep down, that he had been trapped in the tower for too long. He couldn't return to the real world. He didn't want to. What he wanted was for his end to mean something, and for his honour to be restored. With that thought, the Fyreslayer prepared to throw himself in front of the Summoner's attack, perhaps shield his comrades long enough for them to reach the daemon and finish it. Then a flicker of movement caught his eye.

Turning, Sornsson was just in time to raise a hand and block the spinning star of metal that whipped towards him. It dug into his palm, and the flesh smouldered where it struck. Fresh agony raced down Sornsson's arm, and he growled in anger as he caught sight of his assailant. It was the skaven, the one who had given him the poisoned wound in his chest. The damn thing had followed them, even to this last extreme, and was now staring at him in abject horror from a few dozen paces behind.

'Nowhere to run now, is there?' grunted Sornsson. Avanius glanced back, but Sornsson waved him on. 'You take the daemon. I've got the rat.'

The Knight-Questor nodded, and slammed his fist against his chest in salute before turning back to face their nemesis.

From behind him, Sornsson heard a rush of energies as the daemon's magic was unleashed. He heard his companions cry out to their gods, and the air crackling as faith fought sorcery. Too many threats, thought Sornsson grimly, just like before. He couldn't shield them from everything at once. But the sneaking assassin at their backs? That was a threat he could deal with.

Silently wishing his comrades well, the duardin doubled back and bore down on the snarling skaven with a Volturung war cry.

Skrytchwhisker cursed as the stunt-thing caught his throwing star. His aim had been typically perfect, the element of surprise absolute. Obviously the weapon had been defective, and the Deathrunner added its makers to his mental list of victims once he got out of this place. The prize was so close. He had waited while his prey dealt with the daemons, and had intended to let them bear the brunt of the Summoner's magic too before sweeping in to finally claim the daemon's head. Then the stunt-thing had slowed, and Skrytchwhisker had known he needed to deal with that one first. Thanks to the incompetence of others, it seemed he would have to do so at close quarters.

As the duardin accelerated into a lurching charge, the assassin appraised his victim with quick and hungry eyes. Frightening at first glance, this stunt-thing, with its bulging muscles, its glowing runes, and the flames that danced about its body. Yes, frightening enough that lesser skaven would have fled in terror. But Skrytchwhisker was a trained killer, and he saw the rest of the picture. Wounds to the chest, the face, and of course one hand. More cuts and bruises than the assassin cared to count, and a pronounced weakness in the left leg. The skaven allowed himself a smirk. This wouldn't take long.

He allowed his assailant to bear down upon him, waiting

until the last moment to duck nimbly aside. The stunt-thing's axe whistled over Skrytchwhisker's head. In return, the assassin slashed a long, ragged wound across his enemy's ribs with an envenomed blade. The foe-prey gave a curse and wheeled, lashing out with surprising speed. Skrytchwhisker's heart beat a wild tattoo as he flipped back out of harm's way, barely avoiding his enemy's swing. Angry now, the skaven whipped his tail out, regretting momentarily the painful loss of its bladed tip, and wrapped it around the duardin's wrist. A practised twist, and the burly warrior's war pick clattered to the floor, released by nerveless fingers. Skrytchwhisker kicked out with one foot-claw and sent the weapon skidding away across the floor into a fiery trench. His enemy watched the weapon go with something resembling resignation, then hefted his axe and attacked again. Once more, Skrytchwhisker wove aside, flowing like water around the prey-thing's clumsy swings. The Deathrunner permitted himself a moment of triumph as he evaded again, then again, watching his opponent bleeding and tiring by the moment. The time was near. Spinning his blades through his dextrous fingers, Skrytchwhisker prepared to strike the killing blow.

The spell that roared from the Summoner's staff was a whirling vortex of kaleidoscopic flame. It engulfed Avanius and Hathrek in an instant. The hungry energies of unbridled change whirled around the two champions. Avanius saw screaming faces and thrashing limbs flowing through the firestorm, and raised his voice in prayer to the God-King. The flames closed in by the second, and wherever the warriors looked they saw the agonised faces of those they cared about, the blazing ruins of their homes, and the infinite, mind-shattering vistas of Tzeentch's ultimate victory. The heat was unbearable. Avanius felt his flesh scorching as his armour and blade glowed. He could feel the energies of change slithering across his skin like worms, preparing to twist him into some disgusting abomination for the Summoner's amusement. Death held no dread for the Stormcast, for it would mean simply a return to Sigmaron to be reforged once more. But to be transformed in some way, transfigured and trapped here for all time? The Knight-Questor steeled himself, determined to resist such an ignominious fate to the last.

'It cannot end here,' cried Avanius, instinctively raising his denuded shield arm for protection. 'Lord Sigmar, protect your servants!'

'He can't aid us in this place,' bellowed Hathrek. 'But my gods can.'

'Hathrek, no,' shouted Avanius in horror. 'Their gifts are ruin. I would rather die.'

The Darkoath laughed madly at that, the strobing firelight making his face seem inhuman and strange.

'That's fine for you, Avanius,' he spat. 'But not all of us go to the Heavens when we fall.' With that, Hathrek stepped in front of the Knight-Questor, roaring out harsh words in some dark tongue. Once more the skull runes upon his torso blazed with angry red light, and Avanius heard dimly the Summoner's shriek of frustration as his magic faltered. The firestorm tattered apart like clouds before a racing wind. The two warriors were left, standing in a circle of untouched ground, while all around them the floor bubbled and seethed with molten magic. Avanius felt profound shame that it was one of Hathrek's gods, not his, that had saved them. It was as though he had been complicit in something that had left him tainted. Angrily, the Hallowed Knight thrust such thoughts aside. He raised his head to stare at the Gaunt Summoner who loomed atop the dais, and felt a surge of angry gratification as he saw the panic in the daemon's manifold eyes.

* * *

Sornsson was tiring. His wounds were a constant scream of agony that he ignored through willpower alone. But now his body was failing him, and he couldn't ignore that. Only anger kept him going. Anger at himself, for the weakness he despised. Anger at the tower, for all it had put him through. Anger, most of all, at the sneering, lightning-fast vermin that he just could not seem to land a blow on.

Sornsson swung his axe again, but blood loss had made his limbs heavy, and as his runes had gone dark so his strength had lessened by degrees. The blow was sluggish, clumsy, and the skaven stepped contemptuously aside from it with a chitter that sounded suspiciously like laughter. Springing into the air, the ratman lashed out with one foot. It struck Sornsson's left knee with a sickening crunch, and fresh pain exploded up his leg as his kneecap shattered. The Fyreslayer almost blacked out for a moment, feeling it only dimly as the floor rushed up to strike his cheek. Another flash of pain from his wrist and the Fyreslayer watched groggily as the skaven kicked his axe away, his severed hand still wrapped in a death grip around its haft.

Sornsson tried to rise, fighting the tide of pain that was drowning his thoughts. It was no good. He was too broken. Slumping back to the ground, Sornsson watched through a haze as the assassin scurried contemptuously away, stopping some way back from the Summoner's dais. The skaven reached into its robes and drew out a fist-sized device. Brass. Spherical. The duardin's heart beat faster as he saw the creature depress a series of studs in the orb's surface, and his ears rang as it began to emit a high-pitched whine. With horror, Sornsson realised that the assassin had some kind of skaven bomb, and was preparing to hurl it straight into the midst of his comrades. They had survived the Summoner's spell, which was flickering and dying around them. But they wouldn't survive this treachery.

Sornsson heard again the words of the oaths he had sworn. For a split second an image flashed before his eyes, clear as day. Swarming greenskin bodies. Sundered, bloody corpses. Amongst them a fallen figure, forlorn and beyond his aid. The Doomseeker felt the presence of the ring upon one finger of his remaining hand. Slowly, that hand curled into a fist. Then he was pushing himself up, the world spinning around him, the lifeblood running freely from his body. He felt heat on his skin as one last rune still burned between his shoulder blades, bolstering his leg despite its shattered kneecap. Sornsson thanked Grimnir for this last burst of strength as he took first one dragging step, then another. He gathered pace, anger and determination keeping him moving, driving him towards the assassin who was still absorbed with activating the bomb.

The skaven looked up suddenly, verminous features twisting in horror as it saw the Fyreslayer bearing down upon it. For a crucial split second the assassin hesitated, torn between evasion and obvious terror of the explosive device still clutched in one claw. Taking his chance, Sornsson wrapped his arms around his foe and hoisted it bodily off the floor. The bomb was trapped between them, whining towards a crescendo. The skaven went mad with sudden terror, tail and talons lashing as it struggled to escape. Sornsson felt claws rake his thighs. He felt an awful, icy pain as chisel fangs sank deep into his neck. Still he held his grip and kept moving, roaring as he channelled the last of his strength into a stumbling run. Away from his comrades. Protecting them from harm. Fulfilling his oath at last, one way or another. The skaven gave a final, despairing shriek of terror as it realised what Sornsson intended, and then they were plunging headlong into one of the surging rivers of fire that leapt from floor to ceiling. The flames took them instantly, reducing Doomseeker, assassin, and deadly bomb to glowing ashes in a heartbeat.

So fell Vargi Sornsson of the Volturung, his oath fulfilled at last.

Avanius saw the Doomseeker and the Deathrunner plunge together into the flames, and felt a stab of sorrow. It was quickly eclipsed by icy determination as he turned back to look at the Gaunt Summoner. The Knight-Questor strode forwards, Hathrek at his side, the two warriors mounting the steps of the dais with angry, deliberate strides. Before them, the daemon stood and waited, yellow eyes watchful and black tongue slithering about his lips and teeth. As Avanius stepped onto the dais, the Summoner lunged with a ritual dagger. Without breaking stride, the Stormcast whipped his sword around in a furious arc and smashed the weapon from the daemon's hand. Several of the creature's fingers pattered to the floor along with the dagger, and the Summoner recoiled with a hiss. He swung his staff to bear but Hathrek was there, long blade lashing out. The ensorcelled stave broke beneath the blow, its shattered halves bursting into many-coloured flame and vanishing in puffs of ash. The Summoner hissed again, countless eyes bulging in fury, whirling and hunching like a cornered beast. Avanius thought he saw real fear in the daemon's stare for the first time, and felt grim satisfaction. The Summoner backed away until his back bumped against the golden arch, finding two blades pointed straight at his throat.

'On your knees,' snarled Hathrek. Avanius saw a wildness in his companion's eyes. 'Get on your knees and beg.'

Slowly, carefully, the Gaunt Summoner did as he was bid, raising his three hands in a gesture of placation as he knelt.

'Yesss,' the daemon hissed. 'Yesss. You are victorious. I am defeated. My boon issss yours.'

At those words, Avanius shot a warning glance at Hathrek. Now we come to it, he thought. The moment where he would discover if he was worthy of the God-King's trust. The Darkoath stood motionless, muscles taut, but behind his eyes Avanius could see a war being waged.

'Hathrek,' he said. 'You do not want this.'

The chieftain did not respond, gaze fixed upon the daemon that knelt at their mercy.

'Hathrek,' he tried again. 'We have to kill it. The others died so that we could. Would you spit on their deaths by accepting this... thing's gift?'

Hathrek did look round at that, face twisting in fury.

'Why else did I come here, Stormcast? My tribe...'

'Needed their leader,' interrupted Avanius. 'And perhaps they still do. But if you return to them with the Summoner's boon you will bring them only ruin.'

'Nooooooo,' crooned the daemon, tone ingratiating, 'I will give you ssssuch gifts, Hathrek of the Gadalhor tribe. I will make you sssstrong. I will give you the might to avenge your people...'

Avanius saw fear in Hathrek's face then. The Darkoath's head snapped round, and his blade pressed against the daemon's throat, drawing a single bead of oily black blood.

'Avenge?' he demanded. 'I am here to save them!'

Malicious glee blossomed across the Summoner's hideous features at this.

'No,' came his singsong reply. 'You are here to avenge them. Their terrible, painful deathsssss. It stole their souls. Only I can give you the strength to avenge them.' Hathrek looked from the Summoner to Avanius, agony and indecision in his eyes.

'It lies, Hathrek,' cautioned Avanius, seeing the abyss yawning before Hathrek's feet. 'You must kill it. Do not give in to damnation.'

'Why don't you kill it, then, if you're so sure?' spat Hathrek furiously. 'You don't have anything to lose, do you? No people to fear for? Eh? No oaths to keep.'

'I have an oath,' replied Avanius calmly, lowering his blade to his side. 'I swore to defeat the master of the Silver Tower, and so I shall.'

Hathrek scowled in confusion, keeping his own sword at the daemon's neck. The Summoner watched, unblinking, his remaining fingers twitching and twining.

'And you're going to defeat it by putting up your blade?' demanded Hathrek. 'What madness is this?'

Avanius shook his helmed head. 'Defeat. Not slay. I realised the distinction myself only lately, and in that lies a lesson of humility for me. But this is your story, Hathrek of the Gadalhor. It always was.'

'My tribe could be in mortal danger,' gritted Hathrek. 'They could already be dead. Make sense right now, or shut up and stand aside while I claim the power I need.'

'Do that,' replied Avanius, 'and you give this creature precisely what it wants. Your soul. Take its boon and you become its slave. The daemon wins. I realised that my mission was never to slay the Summoner, but to stop it from ensnaring you. There is good in you still, Hathrek. Strength. The potential for greatness. Sigmar has forgiven and accepted worse. Renounce this creature and its lies, give up your quest for power, and I know the God-King will raise you up in glory.'

Hathrek stared at Avanius, searching the Stormcast's eyes for any hint of deception. Avanius stared back, filled with a calm certainty.

'My tribe...' began Hathrek, but the words tailed off.

'This is not about your tribe, Hathrek,' said Avanius sadly. 'This was never, truly, about your tribe. You wanted power for yourself. You wanted to escape the cloying mantle of duty and sacrifice. You wanted – needed – to take action, and claim the strength you thought you deserved.'

Out of the corner of his eye, Avanius could see the Summoner's fingers twitching like the legs of a dying spider. He dared not raise his blade to put an end to whatever mischief the daemon attempted, however, in case he cast aside his one chance to save the Darkoath Chieftain. Slowly, Hathrek's expression darkened with fury.

'And if it was? If I did leave those whining, helpless curs to seek my own glory? If I did seek that which I knew I deserved, not that which my failure of a father laid about my shoulders? How does that give you the right to save me, Stormcast? Why should I turn aside on some nebulous offer of slavery to the God-King, when before me lies the power to become a god myself?' Hathrek's blade swung away from the daemon's throat to hover before Avanius' gorget, but the Stormcast still did not raise his blade.

'It is a false promise, Hathrek. You know this. It is damnation, ruin and slavery. You would not be a god. You would be a monster. Strike me down if you must, but slay this lying creature also, and I will call you brother when next I see you in Sigmaron.'

Avanius watched Hathrek's expression contort with anger, frustration, and fear. Avaricious desire warred with hope, and in that moment the Knight-Questor dared to believe that he might have succeeded in his mission. Then, with a scream, Hathrek raised his blade high between the Stormcast and the Summoner, and swung it down in a single, killing blow.

CHAPTER NINE

LEGEND'S END

Hathrek strode out across the leaping expanse of the crystalline bridge. Behind him loomed the Silver Tower, a cyclopean mountain range of ever-changing architecture and swirling, sorcerous clouds. To either side of him loomed twisted gargoyles of silver and molten flesh, lining the crystal roadway and belching strangely coloured flames into the sky. Below the bridge lay an endless gulf, while above the clouds were tinged rose and gold by the rising of a new sun. Hathrek relished the sensation of fresh air in his lungs, clouds above his head and no walls closing in about him. He felt strong, liberated, victorious.

Ahead of Hathrek, perhaps a mile distant along the impossible bridge, a realmgate spun and swirled. The portal would take Hathrek back to the lands of his tribe, where at last he would claim his fate with his own two hands. Avanius' words had struck a painful chord within Hathrek's heart, forcing him to face truths he had long denied. He had been living in the shadow of his father, the man that had courted the power of the gods in an attempt to protect his tribe. The man that still squirmed and screamed in the iron stockade they had built for him, a bloated thing of bladed tentacles and tumorous flesh, too weak to support the gifts that the Dark Brothers had rained down upon him. Still, Hathrek had sought to continue his labours, to save his tribe not for their sake, but for his.

The Stormcast might have been blinkered by faith, but he had been right about that much at least. Now, Hathrek claimed what he wanted for himself, and if his tribe still lived then they would worship him as the champion his father could never be. They would think him a deity, reflected Hathrek with a fang-filled grin. He certainly looked the part. Where once had walked a mortal man, now there strode a god of war, nine feet tall and clad in flowing armour of silver and blue. A third eye stared from his forehead, yellow and slit-pupiled like that of Hathrek's benefactor, while crystal horns curled from the chieftain's brow. The sword of his father lay discarded in a dusty corner of the tower, forgotten forever. In its place, Hathrek's taloned fists clutched a pair of rainbow-hued blades that shimmered with magical power.

Truly, he thought, he was mighty now in a way that none of his fallen comrades could have even imagined. Avanius, so pious, so convinced that his weakling god was the only true way to power. Sornsson, fleeing his own failures all the way unto death. Eithweil, with all her manipulations and illusions that still hadn't proven enough to overcome the might of Tzeentch. Masudro, so pathetic that he had been slain before the quest had even truly begun. Hathrek could feel them already fading from his mind, irrelevancies discarded in favour of the boundless knowledge that flowed through him. And if he felt sadness at their passing? Loss at their deaths? A twinge of shame at what he had made of their ends? If perhaps some screaming, smothered corner of his mind was certain that everything Avanius had said was true? Those feelings were all fading as well, vanishing like morning mist as Hathrek neared the realmgate which the Summoner had sworn would take him home. A new fate lay before him now, a path upon which such fragments of the past were but chaff to be discarded as the weakness they were.

'I am my own god now,' rumbled Hathrek, feeling the power singing through his veins. 'And I am the master.' With that, the champion of the Silver Tower stepped through the swirling portal, and was gone.

From the twisted safety of his sanctum, the Gaunt Summoner watched the thing that had been Hathrek stride away down the bridge. Within the silvered depths of the Summoner's mirror, a shimmering flow of gold and silver energies stretched away before the former chieftain, while in his wake trailed the severed strands of other, slowly dimming futures. The daemon watched as Hathrek stepped through the realmgate and vanished, going on to whatever end the Changer of the Ways had planned for him. The Gaunt Summoner gave a slow, gleeful sigh. So often, it was the Darkoath Chieftain that took the boon, mused the Summoner, but the harder he struggled, the worthier the final victory. Holding out one hand, the daemon summoned his staff back into reality, the weapon coalescing from swirling clouds of glittering ash. Severed fingers regrew, unnatural energies twining and solidifying into pale blue flesh. It was always important, thought the Gaunt Summoner airily, to make sure his champions believed themselves victorious over him. They had to feel they had earned their reward, or they would become suspicious of some trick. He leered at the irony.

This time it had been close, though. He had almost been slain. These Stormcasts had not been long amongst the realms, but the Summoner found he disliked them and their interference intensely. That one had seen through his ruse, and had almost opened his companion's eyes to the truth. How fortunate, thought the Summoner, that the shadow mage had fallen before their final encounter. She might have detected the cantrips he had used to cloud Hathrek's judgement, the subtle little tweaks of daemonic sorcery that had coaxed all of his negative memories to the forefront of his mind. Still, it was more satisfying to claim those with a shred of good left in their souls, reflected the daemon as he reached into a casket of squealing beetles and popped one daintily into his mouth. He bit down with a crunch, relishing the tiny life he extinguished. Another fate altered by he who was master of them all.

Stepping back from his mirror, the Gaunt Summoner let his eyes roam freely. His pupils stuttered and danced, each moving independently of the others as they sought his next viable prospect. The mirror in which he had watched the champions dulled to blank silver, but as it did so its countless twins flickered with life. Like the compound eye of some monstrous insect, the Summoner's mirrors clustered around one another by the hundred. In each one a different scene of desperation and heroism was depicted, another time and place wherein archetypal champions sought to best the horrors of the Silver Tower. So many legends, so many champions, each band believing they were the only ones.

Here, a brawny barbarian and a nimble aelfen assassin cut their way through throngs of Kairic Acolytes. There a priest of Khorne tumbled, bellowing in rage, from the lip of a crumbling ledge into the endless abyss below. He saw Stormcasts and duardin, humans and aelfs, servants of justice and ambition alike. About each band of potential champions wound shimmering strands, paths of fate that changed hue and texture with every decision the desperate warriors made. The

Summoner watched avidly, seeking the next prospect for the grand scheme.

The daemon was distracted by a chorus of sibilant hissing from high above. Abandoning his search for the moment, the Gaunt Summoner craned his head back and stared into the impossible abyss that stretched away above him. His sanctum had no ceiling. Instead, the space folded outwards, and outwards. Impossible geometries stretched away into the distance, an immensity of fractal spaces fit to obliterate mortal minds at a glance. Amongst that incredible sprawl, the Summoner saw his brethren staring up at him, just as he stared up at them. From their sanctums within their towers, the strange daemons communed for a moment across their labyrinthine dimension.

'How fare you, brother?' came a hissing voice, floating down from on high. The Summoner did not know which of his siblings asked the question. It scarcely mattered; each was the equal of the others, and all were one.

'Another prosssssspect has reached fruition,' he replied with satisfaction. 'Another sssstone has been set to tumbling down the mountainsssside.'

His brothers crooned their pleasure at his words.

'Good,' came the response. 'Good is this. With every day, more send we, siblings dear. Soon they must begin the avalanche.'

'Yessss,' hissed the Summoner venomously. 'Each fate we turn to our own purposes, each champion we lead asssstray... each advancesss the scheme. Each brings us closer to freedom.'

'Freedom,' replied his siblings, and then they were fading, vanishing into the mists of obscurity as they returned to their scrying. The Gaunt Summoner lowered his gaze to his mirrors once more, and his eyes widened in pleasure as he spotted another shimmering golden strand. This one stretched out from a Mistweaver, who even now was using her magic to drive her companions insane. The Summoner watched with rapt attention as the Tenebral Shard drove his blades through the chest of the duardin Doomseeker, then fell to his knees before the Saih with a pleading look upon his face. Already the Slaughterpriest lay dead in the background, his body torn into several pieces. This one, thought the Summoner, drawing the mirror closer to him and craning over it. As he did so he whispered the word once more, enjoying the thrill of it slithering across his tongue.

'Freedom...' Soon, he thought. Soon.

Light blossomed before Hathrek's altered eyes. A racing sensation gripped him, sickening vertigo of the sort he had felt in the tower, and for a terrible moment he wondered whether it had all just been another trick. Then reality unfolded before him, and Hathrek was setting his cloven hooves down upon peaty soil. He breathed deeply, drawing in the familiar scents of the Splintered Hills. The daemon had not lied. He had been returned to his home.

The chieftain looked about, taking in the tangled blackbark trees, the mossy, blade-sharp rocks and the high hillside that rose in a sprawl of daggerthorn bushes to the cloudless night sky above. The stars were known to him, but he felt none of the relief he had expected at that sight. Instead, Hathrek felt only the strength boiling through his veins, the energies of change still finishing their last alterations to his godlike physique. Up there, atop the thornhill, stood his village. His unnatural eyesight picked out the edge of the village stockade, clear as day despite that it stood several miles distant. Shapes moved atop its rampart. Human shapes. So perhaps the Summoner had lied after all, he thought. Perhaps his tribe still lived. Hathrek wasn't sure what he should have felt in that moment, but found himself caring little. He couldn't remember why he ever had.

They should see him though, he thought with a sneer. The wretches for whom he had risked so much should look upon their new god, and swear themselves to him. It was only right. His purpose decided, Hathrek set out towards the village on the hilltop high above, pushing aside stunted black trees as he went.

The first cry of alarm came from the walls when Hathrek was still a hundred yards away. He had been able to see the lookouts on the walls for some time, with their barbarous garb and their vaguely familiar faces. Now, it seemed, their feeble mortal senses had finally detected him, and he tasted their fear upon the air. Hathrek rumbled a cruel laugh, but it was cut short as a volley of arrows rose from behind the stockade and fell towards him. The shafts rained down, shattering against his armour or breaking upon his iron-hard skin. They angered him, all the same, and with a roar Hathrek flexed his newly granted might. Bolts of sorcerous fire roared from his rainbow blades and slammed into the reinforced wooden gate of the village. The structure blew inwards, exploding into a cloud of flying splinters that raised screams of pain from the villagers caught in the blast.

Hathrek grinned to himself, then frowned. This wasn't right. These were his people. A god should not return to his worshippers in such a way. With a gesture, Hathrek raised a shimmering shield of magical energy about himself, and strode on into the place he had once called home.

Nothing had changed. The blazing pitch torches. The squalid, mud-spattered huts and squalid, mud-spattered tribesmen. The bone-pit. The enclosure with its vile, screaming inhabitant. It was all just as Hathrek had left it. In fact, he realised, his eyes narrowing, it was *exactly* as he had left it. Ignoring the screaming villagers who abased themselves or fled in terror, Hathrek lumbered towards the shamans' hut at the centre of the settlement. Sure enough, its hide doorflap was pushed aside and the shamans emerged, his brother at their head. They were daubed in the same runes and markings they had been on the night they sent him along the shadowed paths to the Silver Tower. Because, he knew with absolute certainty, this was that night. How could that be?

Hathrek was gripped by a sudden terrible agony, and everything seemed to shudder and double around him. He staggered, and let out a mighty roar of pain in two voices at once. Through blurring vision, Hathrek saw his brother run forwards, recognition and horror dawning across his features. His brother. The shaman reached out, shouted words. But there was too much pain. Hathrek felt as though he was being pulled in two, as though reality itself were trying to drag him apart. In desperation, he lashed out, instinctively sending his newfound powers roaring through the village of his birth. Tendrils of writhing sorcery exploded from him in every direction, wreathing the villagers and burning them to windblown ash.

Dimly, Hathrek saw his brother recoil in sudden fear, a moment before he was reduced to a shadow that scattered away upon the wind. Hathrek felt new life flowing through him, and he understood then that he had ripped the life force from his tribe to complete his monstrous transformation. Two paths of fate could not exist in one place, and so he had destroyed the old to make way for the new. The Summoner had claimed that something had devoured the souls of his entire tribe, long before he had encountered the daemon in the tower. It had not lied. For a moment, Hathrek felt nothing at all. And then slowly, haltingly, he began to laugh. It was a terrible sound, insanity and pain and hatred and glee all tumbling together and booming out across the hilltop in the pre-dawn light. The dust of dead futures blew about Hathrek in billowing clouds as he rose to his full height, and his third eye opened wide.

'**And why not?**' he demanded out loud to the empty village. '**Why not? I gave them everything. It was their turn!**' The monster that had once been Hathrek roared with laughter once again as he saw that even the enclosure stood empty, nothing but drifting ash coating its floor.

'**I am no longer what you made me, father,**' growled the monster with cruel satisfaction, '**I am not Hathrek, and I do not serve you.**' He looked around at his handiwork, and a terrible grin of madness and malice crept across his features.

'**I am the Soul Eater,**' boomed the daemonic beast to the lifeless hilltop. '**And I serve only Tzeentch.**' With that, the thing that had once been Hathrek of the Gadalhor left the dead remains of his home behind him, and strode away into the darkness.

ABOUT THE AUTHOR

Andy Clark has written the Warhammer 40,000 short story 'Whiteout', the Age of Sigmar short story 'Gorechosen', and the Warhammer Quest Silver Tower novella *Labyrinth of the Lost*. Andy works as a background writer for Games Workshop, crafting the worlds of Warhammer Age of Sigmar and Warhammer 40,000. He lives in Nottingham, UK.